Join Nancy ...

... shakes off the **SHACKLES OF SCHOOL** and gets a **JOB!!**

... develops her very own **THEORY OF DETECTION!**

... investigates **Cook's DARK PAST**

... dreams of getting her **BIG CHANCE** in the movies

... finds out the truth about **ROBBERY, POISON** ... and **MURDER!**

For Lola

NANCY PARKER'S

Diary of Detection

MAIDSERVANTS, MYSTERY AND MURDER!

OXFORD
UNIVERSITY PRESS

Great Clarendon Street, Oxford OX2 6DP
Oxford University Press is a department of the University of Oxford.
It furthers the University's objective of excellence in research, scholarship,
and education by publishing worldwide. Oxford is a registered trade mark
of Oxford University Press in the UK and in certain other countries

Database right Oxford University Press (maker)

First published 2016

British Library Cataloguing in Publication Data

Data available

ISBN: 97-8-019-273938-4

3 5 7 9 10 8 6 4 2

Printed in Great Britain

Paper used in the production of this book is a natural,
recyclable product made from wood grown in sustainable forests.
The manufacturing process conforms to the environmental
regulations of the country of origin.

NANCY PARKER'S
Diary of Detection

by

JULIA LEE

ILLUSTRATED BY CHLOE BONFIELD

OXFORD
UNIVERSITY PRESS

1 THE FUTURE

NANCY'S JOURNAL

My name is Nancy Parker and this is my new Journal. A Journal is not the same as a diary. You don't have to write in it every day, only when you have something you want to say—something important. But I DO have something important to say because:

On this day 24th June 1920 I TURNED FOURTEEN and I LEFT SCHOOL.

Now I am about to step into The Future. How I see the future is like this:

I have tried to explain this Theory to my family without any real sucksess. Except for Aunty Bee who smiles when she listens to me going on.

(I should have put before that I live at 44 Bread Street, London with my Dad and my Grandma and my Aunty Bee. Mum died when I was quite small. I don't know what she'd make of my Theories.)

I think they think for me to have a Theory is nonsense. Even the word THEORY is nonsense when it is anywhere near a girl like me. (I looked it up in the Dictinary at school and made sure I learnt how to spell it.)

About THE FUTURE:

Aunty Bee says 'Who knows what may happen!'

Grandma says I should remember my place and not get above myself.

Dad does not say much at all—but I know he means well.

This Journal was a leaving present from my teacher, Miss Lamb. Main Road Council School is not very big & I've been stuck in the top class for ages. She knew I was SICK TO THE BACK TEETH of doing the same lessons over & over—just waiting for the day when I could leave.

Miss Lamb said that few people lead such exciting lives that they have Something Worthwhile to write down every day. But I plan to have a great many exciting days now that I have thrown off the SHACKLES of SCHOOL!

I am going to write carefully & try my hardest over the spelling—which was always my weak point—because this book is so bieutiful.

(But I think I may already have made a spelling mistake & I do not know whether to cross it out or whether that would spoil it even more.)

When Miss Lamb handed me my present it was beutifully done up in paper and ribbon but I could see it was a book. I thought it might be an improving book like the ones Sunday

School give you for attending every week for a whole year. I have 6 improving books lined up already and I do not need any more. I can scarcely BE more improved.

The books I really like are the 6-penny detective novels Aunty Bee brings back from the Lost Property Office at the Bus Depot. The covers always feature bloody knives— or tall figures with long shadows—or ladies screaming. They are well-thumbed & grubby & people have left them behind on a bus. But I don't care. It is the <u>story</u> that matters. I didn't think Miss Lamb would give me a 6-penny detective novel with a screaming lady on the front. (I don't suppose she has even heard of them.)

I know that in The FUTURE I could not be a teacher— you need exams for that & Main Road Council School was not the place for passing exams—or a <u>Bus Conductress</u> like Aunty Bee. (They are not taking on any Females these days. 'They were glad enough of women during the War, weren't they?' she always says. But now the men need their jobs back & there are more men asking than there are jobs to give them.) But Aunty Bee enjoys the work—even tho she's on her feet all day running about taking everyone's fares—and the uniform is very smart.

These are the jobs I would like to do & would be good at:—

1. Acting on the stage or in films.

My experiense has mainly been in the Sunday School Nativity Play. I was usually a shepherd or a person in the

9

crowd and once I was the Inn-keepers wife. I can ACT all right but they never pick someone with frizzy ginger hair to be an Angel.

2. In a shop.

Altho this is not <u>IDEAL</u> I wouldn't mind working in one where you wear a smart black dress & sell interesting things. I don't wish to work on a Greengrocers stall & get chapped hands like Ethel Boyd who left school at Christmas. Or a butchers shop. (I hate the sawdust on the floor that starts out white and turns dark brown where the blood drips on to it from the cuts of meat.)

3. A Detective.

This is what I would <u>most</u> like to be. I cannot think of any reason why I could not be one. Except perhaps I am too young. And I don't like blood.

What I <u>DON'T</u> want to do is work at the Biscuit Factory like nearly everyone else round here & come home—worn out—with my clothes & hair smelling of biscuits. Now I am being called downstairs.

(I AM WRITING THIS BIT LATER ON)

Aunty Bee bought a cake from the bakers for my birthday. She said it was to save Grandma the trouble of making me one. Then she whispered in my ear—Save us the trouble of eating it too! (Grandma's cakes always taste of odd things like Cough Medicine or cabbage.) (Cooking is not Grandma's favourite task.)

My other presents were—

* New shoes which I need badly. I knew about these as I had to try them on at the shop last Saturday.
* A brand-new detective novel from Aunty Bee. (Not one from Lost Property!)
* A big bag of broken biscuits from Dad. He works at the Biscuit Factory (not making and packing biscuits—the girls & women do that). He looks after the machinery and keeps it running. I know I put that I don't want to work there & come home smelling of biscuits. But I don't mind that he does. Specially on the days they make the Cinnamon Squares (my favourites).

I did not show this Journal to anyone downstairs even though it is so beautiful with its red cover & gold-edge pages. I want to keep it Secret & if they knew about it they'd only want to look inside. So I will have to hide it in my drawer under my clothes and only write in it when no one is about. Aunt Bee & me share the back bedroom so it is going to be tricky.

I can hardly bileve I have written 5 pages. At school it would be TORTURE to write 1.

I have to finish this before Aunt Bee comes up to bed. That is why my handwriting is not as tidy as I wished but at least I have not done any crossing-out yet or even a

2 DAGGERS DRAWN

Fifty miles away from Bread Street two children glared at each other across a wide stretch of grass that was called, rather unadventurously, The Green. Even though they didn't know each other, they might as well have been sworn enemies with daggers drawn.

The boy had a moon face and horn-rimmed specs, which he hated. He peered out round the hedge that bordered the vicarage garden. His name was Quentin Ives, and he hated that, too. He wished he had a more dashing name. In fact he had invented one: John Horsefield. John Horsefield was an Alias, his undercover name. No one had yet called upon Quentin to risk his life for his country on Top Secret business, but he was ready.

The girl who stared back at him was called Eleanor Mary Otter, but everyone knew her as Ella. Ella was perfectly happy with her name, both the long and the short versions. She was small and square, with straight black hair like a Japanese doll, and she too wore specs. Now she squinted her eyes up in the afternoon sunshine and thought, 'That. Is. The Boy.'

She knew who The Boy was, of course, even if she didn't know his name yet. There was very little that went on around The Green that she didn't know about. In fact, there was very little that went on around The Green at all.

Ella knew that the boy lurking in the hedge had been sent to stay with the vicar, Mr Cheeseman, because he was hopeless at school. He had come bottom of his class in almost everything and the school didn't want him back unless he worked harder. So he was going to have to spend his summer holidays doing extra lessons to show that he could improve.

Ella felt rather smug. She had never been to school. Her father, an expert in Archaeology, taught her at home, along with various people he engaged for the subjects he did not personally excel at. Recently Professor Otter had decided that Ella was ready for a new challenge and had put her in for the entrance exam for the Girls' Grammar School. Ella passed with flying colours; she was due to start there in September, along with all the other new eleven-year-olds. Over the summer her father was allowing her a break from lessons, apart from making an Anthropology Scrapbook—that is, studying the customs and habits of a tribe. Ella had wanted to keep a scrapbook about a jungle tribe, but her father said it had to concern people she could actually observe and study. So it really had to be the inhabitants of Seabourne, the town where she lived. She was to make notes, draw maps, and snip bits out of the local paper. This hardly counted as work, according to Professor Otter. He loved learning and couldn't understand why anyone would want a break from it. Ella, however, welcomed the idea of a holiday; it would make her more like other children.

But after only a day or so time was hanging heavy.

There wasn't enough to do, and there was no one much to do it with. What she really needed were some friends. Not that this boy looked the sort she'd want to associate with . . . as far as she could tell.

She nipped back indoors. Her father was at his desk, deep in thought. His spectacles rested halfway down his dear old beaky nose. A pen sat forgotten in his hand and there was an ink stain on his forehead.

'D'you mind if I borrow the binoculars, Father?'

'Um . . . no, of course not. What do you want them for?'

'Close-up observation,' said Ella, and ran out again.

Quentin Ives was an only child. His mother was an impatient woman who often called people nincompoops, and his father was a short-tempered man who thought everyone but himself was bird-brained. So when Quentin started at boarding school last autumn he found himself calling the other boys nincompoops and bird-brains. This didn't make him any friends. And when his work was marked, and the results were read out to everyone, it became clear that the greatest nincompoop and bird-brain in the class was Quentin himself. Which came as a bitter blow and a complete surprise to him.

He tried to tell his parents he wasn't cut out for boarding school but they just told him, 'Nonsense!'

So it was a great relief when the end of the summer term came, and the end of the school year. He longed for home—with no other boys in it, no children at all—for his own comfy bedroom, and familiar food, and his parents mostly out of the way about their own business. Instead, to his horror, he was sent straight off to a tutor for yet more lessons! Quentin's idea of a summer holiday was suiting himself: lying on the sunny lawn or in the cool shade of his room, reading comics and adventure stories, and turning every so often to the magically-refilled tray by his side for a drink of lemonade or another ham sandwich. And after that, perhaps, undertaking a thrilling adventure of his own.

But Mr Cheeseman had already worked out a strict programme of study, and Mrs Cheeseman looked the sort who didn't like you sneaking off to your bedroom at every chance. At least there were no other children in the house. Quentin feared that Mrs Cheeseman might think he was lonely. She'd want to introduce him to the neighbours' children or, even worse, invite them to tea. If he was lucky there wouldn't be any neighbouring children of his age.

He decided to spy out the area straight away. *John Horsefield knew it was essential to be well-informed about The Enemy.* From his bedroom, from the high landing windows, and from behind the front hedge, he carefully surveyed The Green and all its houses. The sea couldn't be far away, but there was no sound, or smell, or sight of it from The Green. It could have been any quiet, comfortable village anywhere in England. But—it was a point always made in the adventures he read—you should never rely on appearances.

Quentin made thorough mental notes:

Ancient cottage with thatched roof—old lady spotted in garden, along with hens, and a small brown donkey. No children.

Square house built like a miniature castle—military-looking old gentleman striding about, flicking worm-casts off the lawn with the end of his stick. No children.

Large white villa—two young ladies sitting on swing-seat, chatting and laughing. Not old enough to have children, though perhaps old enough for a baby or two. (Babies did not worry Quentin.)

One house with no activity at all.

Which left only the red house with the high white gable on the far side of The Green. It was here—when he looked out from behind the hedge—that he saw That Girl. Standing bold as brass in the gateway, staring back at him. He drew his head in quickly.

After a carefully timed two minutes Quentin peeped out again. She was still there. Still gazing in his direction—and now she had something in her hand. Binoculars! She raised them to her eyes and levelled them at him, like an ornithologist fixing on a rare bird.

Quentin dived into the hedge. It smelled of cats. Mr Cheeseman had seemed proud of his garden when he showed Quentin around, and very proud of this huge hedge of yellow-spotted laurel. But it made a good hiding place, despite the fact that it was stinky and scratchy and the leaves looked as if someone had sicked up custard all over them.

He consulted his wristwatch. For four and a half minutes precisely he crouched there. Four and a half minutes was long enough to make people think that you had gone away. *Silently, stealthily, John Horsefield crept from his hiding place.* On hands and knees, he reached the end of the hedge. That Girl, if she was still watching, would not be looking for him down there. He peeped out.

A large ginger cat, just inches away, peered back at him. When it saw that he was just a boy, not something good to catch and eat, it gave him a withering look and strolled off.

That Girl was no longer in her gateway.

'Quentin Ives!' thundered the voice of Mr Cheeseman. 'What are you up to, boy? Get up at once, and come here!'

3 THE EARLY BIRD CATCHES THE WORM

NANCY'S JOURNAL

I have got a <u>JOB</u>!!
Now The Future looks like this:

I am going to be a General Maid. This is not at all what I had in mind but as Aunty Bee says, 'it is A Start In Life'. Only a day ago I was a schoolgirl dying of boredom & now I will be bringing in a <u>wage</u>.

I shall write the whole story down as it is another Momentous Thing that has happened to me. (I am rather happy with the way this Journal is going so far!)

Last night we looked at the SITUATIONS VACANT page in Aunty Bee's evening paper. There was nothing on the stage or in shops. Nor in a Detective Agency. Not even for a person with age and experiense.

The only SITUATIONS VACANT seemed to be for servants.

I felt quite Cast Down. But Aunty Bee underlined the jobs she felt I could apply for. 'You never know what might come of it,' she said. And Grandma said, 'The early bird catches the worm. So you get out there sharpish tomorrow morning, my girl!'

So I did.

With the result that I am to work for a lady called Mrs Bryce who lives at 11 St Alban's Row—which takes 2 bus-rides to get to. I applied at a couple of places before that but I got turned away. The 1st time by a bald man in a shiny black waistcoat who took one look at me and said, 'The post is taken. And next time—go round the back!' & shut the door right in my face. (It was a very shiny black door too.)

At the 2nd house I did go round the back & found a big woman beating the life out of a carpet. Her arms were just like cooked hams. She took one look—they only seem to need one—and said I was too young & too skinny for what they wanted. I stood there in a cloud of carpet-dust trying not to ~~couhf~~ cough while she told me everything that was wrong with me. I needed to be at least 16—and strong—and have some Prior Experiense.

How can you get experiense when you've only just left school?

I was somewhat fed-up! I had been on 3 buses already trying to find my way about in strange ~~nay knee~~ neighbourhoods. My new shoes were rubbing my heels. It was a very warm day & I know I go all pink when I get hot. My frock that I'd carefully ironed was crumpled & my hands were so sticky the print was coming off the bit of newspaper Aunty Bee had cut out for me.

So then I tried the last address on it—which by then I could hardly read. It was not nearly so grand as those other places. St Alban's Row is an ugly old terrace with no front gardens & no way to go round to the back door that I could see. As I got near No. 11 a very pert girl of at least 16 was coming down the steps and she gave me such a look! Like she'd just got the job. Or if not—then she knew I wouldn't get it either.

I still knocked at the door (which was not shiny at all). It turned out to be Mrs Bryce herself who opened it.

She was NOTHING like I expected. I suppose I'd pictured someone like Mrs Vokes who runs the Sunday School: frosty face, grey hair, huge chest dangling with black beads. (Mrs Vokes is the only posh person I know.) But this Mrs Bryce was young. She was smiling. She asked me inside! At first I thoght her dress was very plain but soon I realized that it was very MODERN.

Since I'd actually got past the door I wasn't going to mess up this chance—so I said in my best acting voice, 'My name is Nancy Parker. I've just left school but I have plenty of experiense in running a household. My grandma taught me everything.'

(Not quite true. Grandma has her own way of running our house & doesn't ~~bileve~~ belive anyone else can do it as well as she can. The only things she trusts me to do are easy tasks like peeling potatoes & making beds. She always says, 'Life is nothing but HARD WORK'. But really she has spoilt me.)

'I'm strong' I said. I showed her my hands. They looked a bit soft for someone who is meant to be used to household chores. A bit sweaty too.

Then I got in quick with, 'I can't give you a reference from any previous employer but you can write to my teacher Miss Lamb at Main Road Council School. She will tell you I am helpful and hard-working.'

I remembered to be polite & say 'M'm' after everything. Aunty Bee warned me about that: Lady employers like you to call them M'm. You mustn't baa it out—Ma'am. Neither should you sound like you swallowed a plum and say Modom. They do that in posh shops & it just sounds silly. (I don't know when Aunty Bee has ever been in a posh shop!)

Mrs Bryce was still smiling. She asked my age & a few other things like had I ever worked before—I repeated that I'd only just left school—and then she gave me a funny look as if she was adding up a sum or something. Next she said, 'Have you a mother?' That was a surprise. But then I never went up for a job before so maybe they always ask that. I didn't want to tell her about losing my Mum so I just shook my head.

Next she asked, 'A father?' I told her Dad worked at the Biscuit Factory. I said he had been in the War because I didn't want her to think he wasn't a hero too. But he hasn't really been the same since he came back. (That's

21

how Grandma always puts it. I know it's true. I just wish I hadn't blurted it out like that to some posh lady I barely knew.)

She went on to say that they were not a big household. There was just her & her little dog—and she cast such a sad look at a photo on the mantelpiece of a man in uniform. I knew it must be her husband & he must have DIED IN THE WAR. So then I didn't feel so bad about mentioning Dad.

SURPRISE SURPRISE, I got the job!

I start first thing on Monday. Live-in, with every Sunday afternoon free once luncheon is cleared away. Luncheon! I ask you!! There is a Cook who will do the cooking and I will have to do everything else. I hope Mrs Bryce won't be ~~disp~~ diserpointed in me. I am v. quick to learn.

But then I can't really see why she chose me. My Theory—which I worked out on the bus home—is that she thinks I will be easy to manage because I am YOUNG & IGNORANT. (I am certainly ignorant of housekeeping.) And because I am CHEAP. You don't have to pay youngsters with no Prior Experiense as much as older girls. It didn't look like Mrs Bryce has as much cash swishing about as those other places.

I did pluck up my courage & ask about that girl I saw leaving but Mrs Bryce told me 'She didn't suit—too brash and impertinent, that one'.

As Gran would say 'Too clever by half'. (She often says that about me.)

4 WORST FEARS

Quentin's worst fears were about to be realized. He staggered out of the vicar's study after a whole hour of geometry, and headed for the garden. Mrs Cheeseman caught him. 'Quentin! In here, if you please.'

Here was the sitting room. It was full of females—on the sofa, in the armchairs, on the footstool: females everywhere! Beyond the French windows Quentin could see the sunny lawn and freedom, but it was not to be.

Mrs Cheeseman introduced him to the other guests. 'Miss Dearing, who lives at Apple Cottage.'

That was the old lady with the hens and the donkey, Quentin thought. She wore the same peculiar purple hat.

'Mrs Finch, and her daughters, Penelope and Popsy.'

The two young ladies who'd sat on the swing-seat and giggled. They were giggling now. Quentin suspected they were giggling at him. They were laughing about his name, or his specs, or his face, which was going fiery red—he could feel it. And feeling it only made it worse: he was blushing because he could feel himself blushing! He would never make a real undercover agent. John Horsefield had to be cool as a cucumber. Not red as boiled beetroot. He turned away.

Only to find That Girl.

'And here we have Ella Otter,' said Mrs Cheeseman. 'Ella is terribly clever! It's only to be expected, of course. She's the daughter of Mildmay Otter, the eminent archaeologist. It's a pity your father couldn't join us, Ella. But then Professor Otter never accepts an invitation to tea. He has far more important things to do.'

That Girl scowled fiercely. She crouched on the footstool, her feet tucked awkwardly beneath it. The green dress she wore had a dirty mark down the front. Her black fringe was cut straight across her forehead and she had on small wire-rimmed specs. It was important to notice details, Quentin told himself; you never knew when you might be called on to remember them.

Mrs Cheeseman went on, 'Professor Otter is an American, but he came here to study many years ago because he loves ancient things, and America didn't have enough ancient things in it. What is that amusing story he tells, Ella?'

That Girl scowled even more fiercely, and didn't reply. Quentin knew she hated being there just as much as he did.

'The professor says that the most ancient building in the town where he grew up was only ten years older than him. Imagine that, in England!' Mrs Cheeseman laughed at her own words, then clapped her hands. 'Tea, everyone?'

Mrs Finch patted the cushion next to her. Quentin pretended he hadn't seen and perched on the piano stool, as far from the Finches as he could get. Miss Dearing offered him cake. If he had to be imprisoned here for the next hour or so he would make the most of it. He took the largest slice, and noticed that Miss Dearing helped herself to the next largest.

Mrs Finch shook her head at cake and said, with a gleam of excitement, 'Does anyone else know about Major Corcoran's frightful robbery?'

Robbery? Quentin almost choked.

That Girl was staring at Mrs Finch. It looked as if the robbery was news to her, too. Mrs Finch went on, 'Popsy heard it—didn't you?—from one of our maids. Several items snatched from right off the major's desk.'

Miss Dearing shuddered. 'Please, let's not even think about such a ghastly topic.'

Mrs Cheeseman agreed. 'We won't spoil a delightful party. Now, how do you take your tea, Quentin? Milk? Sugar?'

'Please,' he mumbled, mouth full, 'have you got any lemonade?'

Free at last, Ella ran. She did feel just a little bit sorry for The Boy. At least she could escape from the vicarage and Mrs Cheeseman's clutches, while he was stuck there for the whole summer. He didn't look too thrilled at the prospect. The only time he brightened up was when the robbery was mentioned.

A robbery! Ella thought. A true crime, here, on her doorstep. She had to find out more. She would make a detour past Major Corcoran's house right now, to see if there was anything to observe and make notes about.

As she started across The Green, Ella spotted a strange car drawn up outside Cliffe Lodge, the house next door to her own. A driver in a peaked cap sat inside. She slipped behind the big oak tree so that she could watch without being seen. The motor car was a stylish model in gleaming shades of caramel and cream, much smarter than any vehicle usually seen around The Green. Mr Finch drove a dull black roadster, the vicar rode a shabby bicycle, and Miss Dearing had her beloved donkey cart, painted a gaudy fairground red and yellow.

Cliffe Lodge was usually rented out but no one had lived there in months. Ella was used to roaming its lawns and paths and shrubberies as if they were her own. She had peered through all the downstairs windows and picnicked in the summerhouse. From the far end of the garden she could get on to a path which led to the cliffs and the sea. At the end of her own garden there was just a meadow where a farmer kept a bad-tempered bull. Ella thought of herself as fearless, but she would never dare cross a field with a bull in it.

But now it looked as if Cliffe Lodge was to be let out again. She was just wondering if she could find out more from the driver of the motor car when the front door opened. Two people stepped out: an elegant-looking woman and a man she recognized as the house agent from Seabourne. Drat it! Ella thought.

After a few moments' talk—she was too far away to hear any of it—they shook hands and the man hurried away. The woman strolled over to the sleek motor, said something to the driver, and then sauntered along the lane which bordered the Green. In her delicate shoes and smart frock she looked exactly the type to take a house for the summer. The Green was at the quiet end of Seabourne, away from the racy seaside attractions the day-trippers flocked to, but near enough to the promenade and the plush hotels.

Ella sneaked after her, keeping out of sight, as far as the church. The churchyard was another place that she thought of as her own territory. It was sad in a romantic sort of way, with leaning tombstones and an ancient gateway with a tiled roof, called a lychgate. As the woman reached the lychgate, a tall figure appeared from the churchyard. The woman joined him in the shadow beneath the roof. They leaned close and talked urgently. There was something shifty about the pair of them. Ella felt her heart beat faster. First, news of a robbery, and now this. At last, interesting things were happening at The Green!

5 I BEGIN MY CAREER

NANCY'S JOURNAL
<u>11 St Alban's Row</u>

Well! I arrived all keen & eager only to find that Mrs Bryce is away and there was just the Cook & a little dog here. Cook is called Mrs Jones. She's tall & bony & her face is as grim as a hangman's. I sort of expected a cook to be plump & jolly & smell of custard. This one smells of Carbolic soap.

Pity that Mrs Bryce isn't here—she was so nice and ~~simp~~ symperthetic when I met her. Cook is quite sharp in her manners. I hope I shan't be miserable here. Or lonely. Tho there is THE DOG for company.

I know he is a Sausage Dog, or Dash-hound, which is a German breed of dog. (I remember it was much hated in the War.) (Anything German was hated. If people owned a Dash-hound they used to keep them out of sight.)

He followed me about all morning looking droopy eyed like this:

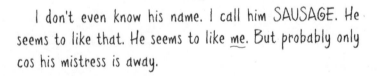

I don't even know his name. I call him SAUSAGE. He seems to like that. He seems to like <u>me</u>. But probably only cos his mistress is away.

I am writing this in my bedroom. It is down in the gloomy old Basement, next to the kitchen. I never had a room to myself before. Me and Aunty Bee have shared the back bedroom at Bread Street for years.

I found my uniform laid out on the bed:-

Cook took one look at my shoes & said, 'I suppose they'll do'. My new shoes! She is a grumpy sort.

The dresses are loose on the waist & short in the hem. They must have come from the previous girl. (I wonder what happened to her?) I am supposed to let the hems down myself. (Haha—they have not seen my sewing yet!)

I put the lacy cap on as best I could. When I came out Cook sneered, 'You're only cleaning. You won't need that fancy thing on!' & handed me a big old cap like a duster which covers all my hair.

She sent me upstairs with a broom & a great heavy box of cleaning things to see to the front room, all the stairs & landings, and Mrs Bryce's bedroom. This was very untidy with lovely clothes just flung about everywhere. Aunty Bee would die for silk stockings & petticoats like those.

I have never worked so hard in ALL MY LIFE!

So now I wear a uniform & am run off my feet just like Aunty Bee. Except that she can make jokes with the passengers & I just get sad silent looks from a dog.

Cook called me for dinner after that—except she calls it LUNCH. Because the Missis is away it was just sandwiches. It's surprising how tasty sandwiches can be even when made by someone with a hard face & a grim expression. (They were ham & mustard.)

I thought Cook might tell me something about herself. But she is not the chatty sort. Far from it.

I did say in a casual sort of tone, 'Oh, what happened to the last girl, then?' Cook snapped back, 'We'll have NO GOSSIP in this house! The missus can't abide it. And nor can I!' Then she shut her mouth so hard I swear I heard her jaws crack together.

After the sandwiches & two pots of tea she went off to her room clutching the newspaper. The front page headline read HUMAN FOOT FOUND IN COAL CELLAR. (I would like to read the rest of that story.) So I came into my room too, since I had no more instrucktions.

My room is DARK despite the sunny day outside. The breeze keeps knocking some ivy against the window. I was going to go on with my new Detective Book—'Murders In The Mist'—but I've got to the part where a woman in a lonely house thinks she hears someone creeping about outside & I suddenly didn't feel like reading. What with the ivy tapping & the wind rattling the glass. St Alban's Row is far from lonely—& I can hear Cook SNORING right through the wall. But all the same.

So I'm writing instead.

The door to my room has just crept open a few inches! All by itself.

I am sure I shut it.

It ISN'T Cook because I can still hear her snoring.

No one has come in. I am just sitting here waiting for what happens next. Writing it down in case it is the LAST THING I ever do!!

Somebody has come in. It was THE DOG! He must have pushed it open with his nose. I am still shaking which is why my writing looks SO BAD.

But I cannot really blame poor Sausage. He is so very lonely and sad.

The Space For Writing Messages

Tuesday
Dear Dad, Grandma
& Aunty Bee,
Just to let you know all is well so you don't have to worry! I am working hard and getting on just fine. You would be proud of me, Grandma. I have my own little room and the meals are nice.

Post Card

Tho not as nice as yours, of course! Cook is all right and the dog is frendly. I am looking forward to seeing you all on Sunday afternoon.

With all my love, Nancy x

(Friday) Dear All –

Had to write this on a sugar bag that Mrs Green next door was kind enuff to find. I knew Dad & Aunty Bee would be at work at this hour but I did hope Gran would be home. Or left the key in the Usual Place so I could get indoors. I waited as long as I could but Mrs Bryce said she could not spare me for long as my afternoon off is not due yet. Now I have got to dash to catch my bus. The news is that Mrs Bryce has taken a house at the coast & we are off tomorrow & it is all a mad rush packing up one house & moving to the next which will be:—

Cliffe Lodge, The Green, Seabourne, Sussex.

This was as much a SURPRISE to me as it will be to you. I wish she had menshunned it before. So I shan't be able to come home on Sundays. I will write again soon. I miss you all very much. But it is a great chance to be at the seaside for the summer & not just for a day trip.

Goodbye!

Love from Nancy x

6 ALL MOD CONS

NANCY'S JOURNAL
Cliffe Lodge, The Green, Seabourne

I can't beleve the W.C. here! It is something like a King might use, with a little step up to reach the Throne. White china & wood panelling & a window of misty glass so no one can see in—or out. And that is just for the SERVANTS. The one upstairs for Mrs Bryce to use has flowers & birds all over it!

I know it is daft to write about the W.C. before anything else. But if all you've had is a dark little outside privy (like at St Alban's Row) or—worse!- a privy in the yard shared with all the neybours & always VERY STINKY (what we've got at Bread Street) then it is thrilling.

Cliffe Lodge is much newer than St Alban's Row and has all Mod. Cons. which Cook says means modern conveniences. She thinks the kitchen very superior. It's on the ground floor with a view over the ~~vedge~~ vegtable garden & our bedrooms are 2 floors up. No dark dingy basement at all! (Tho Cook doesn't like being so far from her kitchen.)

There's a GREAT DEAL of house to keep clean. I shall be run off my feet. But I must find time to keep this Journal going—I have so many Momentous Things to put in it. (I'm writing in pencil today to be quick & not make blots.) There's only me sleeps in my bedroom but I still hide it away under my clothes in the drawer. I have written

34

things I would not like Cook to read!

I must add a bit about our journey down here yesterday.

Mrs Bryce hired a Motor Car & driver. I never rode in one before. (Plenty of buses & trams + the odd train, but not a motor car!) Mrs Bryce sat in comfort in the back with Sausage. Cook had gone earlier on the train with the luggage. I was stuck up front next to the driver, my little cardboard suitcase on my knees.

The driver wore a peaked cap & leather gloves with cuffs like wings. He looked very young to be driving such a grand motor car—nothing like as old as Dad (who I know to be 37). I felt most awkward sitting just inches away from some Young Man I never met before, wondering when a bump in the road would throw me into his lap. But he was a good driver & it never happened. Once we were out of London I found I was enjoying myself. There isn't the view you get from the top deck of a bus but it was still marvellous to see the countryside going by, mile after mile.

Turns out he's from where we are now (Seabourne) where his uncle runs a Garage. He told me his name— Alfred Lubbock—& that he's only just 17 & this is his first showfer job. Usually he is under a car fixing it—he laughed when he said that! I asked what a showfer was and he told me it was a FANCY FRENCH WORD for a driver. He even spelled it for me but of course I couldn't write it down just then. I told him it was my first job too. We got on all right after that.

Alfred Lubbock is just as easy going with Cook as he

was with me. As we sat round the kitchen table he said, 'Well, Mrs Jones,' (I had quite forgotten she had any name besides Cook) 'these are very fine scones indeed! The lightest I ever tasted. My own dear mother's are not a patch on these.'

I expected Cook to tell him not to be cheeky or even box his ears. But she didn't do any such thing. (She took a glass of cooking sherry while we drank our tea as she said it had been a long old day—I don't know if that had anything to do with her good mood.) She said, 'It's nice to be ~~aper~~ appreeshiated' & nudged the plate towards Alfred so he could take another. Which he did. 'You'd be welcome in the kitchen of a swanky hotel with baking like that,' he told her.

Cook looked modest & told him that she had known Mrs Bryce for years & would not dream of leaving. Next Alfred asked 'Why is that, then?' His voice was still cheeky but his face went all serious & symperthetic—and Cook was taken in. She said, 'I used to work for her mother. The family were very kind to me at a hard time. I promised I would look after the Missus when she was young and flighty—Mrs Treadgold as she called herself in those days—& so here I am & here I will stay.'

You could have knocked me down with a feather! I know I've only been here a few days but Cook's never said anything of a PERSONAL NATURE in that time. Now here she was blabbing away to a stranger.

I was wondering what she meant by A HARD TIME when Alfred piped up 'What became of Mister Treadgold then?' I nearly kicked him under the table on his great lanky shins. Except he'd asked when I didn't dare—and I wanted to hear the answer. (I'd like to know about Mr Bryce too.)

But then it was back to usual. 'I'm forgetting myself' Cook said through gritted teeth. 'That's none of your blooming business!' & her face shut up like a clam.

She pulled the plate of scones away & packed me off to do the washing-up with one of her hellish glances. But it was more than I had got out of her in a whole week working close together & Alfred Lubbock had just 1/2 an hour.

He'd make a better DETECTIVE than me. When all he wants to do is fix cars!

TOWER BRIDGE, LONDON

-Post Card-

Nancy — we are all heartbroken that you are so far away from us! But at least you have not been whisked away to the Dark Satanic Mills or up on the Rain-Soaked Moors! No — you are at the seaside, along with all the buckets & spades & donkeys & pierrots! That is where your glittering career has taken you already!! Send us a big stick of rock.

Your Dad and Grandma send their love, & mine,

From your
Aunty Bee

Dear All,

Well, here I am. The new house is ever so grand—you should see it! We are not on the seafront—which is a bit disserpointing—but in the countryside just out of town. So I've not seen any donkeys or pierrots. But I have seen the sea. There's a path that leads there over the golf links. I was worried the golfers would shout at me but nobody did (this time). The sea looked a long way down! The cliff path takes you to Seabourne town if you follow it far enough. But I had only nipped out quickly & I had to be back in time to lay the table for dinner.

Must tell you—there is an air-o-plane which flies over every day pulling a red banner that says VISIT SUNNY SEABOURNE!

I know why it is said to be healthy at the Coast. The air is always so fresh here—it makes your head spin! Even the milk tastes different. And it is so quiet (apart from the birds which are noisy.) I've got a nice room to myself up on the top floor. There are 3 bedrooms for staff but Cook only slept there one night & then moved down to a tiny room beside the kitchen becos she did not like being so far away!

There's <u>LOADS</u> to do. One job is to walk Sausage twice a day. We just go round the green and that is quite enuff for his short legs. Some of the naybours nod

Good Day but others just stare—in particular a rude boy who peeps round corners. But they say people in the countryside are a bit simple so that must be it.

But despite all I have managed to finish 'Murders In The Mist' & just begun 'Scream Blue Murder' which is very gripping.

What a long letter! Love to you all,

Nancy

P.S. Would you say being married twice is a lot of times when you are Mrs Bryce's age? (About the same as Aunty Bee.) It is not important—just something I am wondering about.

P.P.S. If you think this writing paper & envelope look a bit posh it is becos I had to borrow them from Mrs Bryce. She has not paid me my wages yet so I could not buy any for myself. (Nor have I been any place where I could buy them.)

44 Bread Street, London S.E.

Dear Nancy,

I wrote this in a sealed letter and not a postcard this time as I have to say — and your Gran and your Dad are with me too — when you say 'borrowed' did you mean nicked?? Did you nick that fancy notepaper off your employer's desk? Do take care, Nancy! You've a good job there and must not trifle with it. I dare say she has paid your wages by now so you are out of that pickle. Send us a postcard next time. A nice view of the pier! Is there a pier at Seabourne?

I've got a couple more of those crime novels you like — one's a real Lulu! I will parcel them up and send them on.

All well here and everything just as usual. Do try and put your feet up sometimes.

All the best,
 From your loving Aunt

Grandma and Dad send their love too. XX

P.S. What a funny question about Mrs Bryce being married a lot. Good luck to her if she is my age & has been married twice!

7 MORE LESSONS LEARNT

Quentin had spent the day indoors, working. His lessons took place in Mr Cheeseman's study, which commanded a clear view of the gateway and the broad gravel drive up to the front door. The hedge of spotted laurels hid everything else, and hid the vicarage from inquisitive eyes. It also made the study very dark. Heavy floor-length curtains made it even darker. Mr Cheeseman's desk was tucked back in the shadows. Quentin soon realized that while the vicar could see out perfectly well, it was hard for anyone outside to see in and spot him.

The vicar had a great many callers, so that Mrs Cheeseman was always scurrying along the worn hall carpet to answer the door. Sometimes Mr Cheeseman would leap up before she could get there, poke his head out and say, 'Tell them I cannot be disturbed. We are in the middle of a Latin lesson.' He always said Latin lesson, even if it was History or Mathematics. Quentin thought Latin lesson must sound more important than any other subject, something it was impossible to interrupt. The front door would open and close, and then Mrs Cheeseman would say, 'All clear, dear!' But a few callers insisted on waiting until the Latin lesson was over.

Right now they were doing Geography. Or, rather,

Quentin was struggling with Geography and across the huge desk Mr Cheeseman was struggling with the Sunday sermon he had to write. There weren't even any callers to save them. Quentin gazed about the room, his mind an utter blank. The walls were covered with framed photographs, mostly of a much younger Mr Cheeseman and friends in sportswear, holding bats and balls and cups and shields. Quentin could pick out Mr Cheeseman easily—he was always the tallest. Rowing, fencing, rugby, tennis; even a group in mountain-climbing gear, with snowy peaks behind them. Was there nothing Mr Cheeseman hadn't tried?

Quentin loathed sport in general and team sports in particular. He was hopeless at them. At boarding school he'd found that out in no time at all. In fact, it was the fastest bit of learning he'd ever done. (Not that you won any points for that kind of lesson.) Big heavy balls always landed in his face or his stomach. Small hard balls smashed him in the fingers and bashed him on his toes. He never managed to catch them first. He swished and lashed with bats and sticks and racquets but nothing got hit except his team-mates, which didn't help. The games master just yelled, 'Ives! What do you think you're doing!?' But if Quentin knew that, he wouldn't have done it in the first place.

He gazed at a young Mr Cheeseman, above the mantelpiece, beaming and holding up an enormous silver cup garlanded with ribbons. There was no sign of what he had won it for. Just general being-awfully-good-at-games.

'Quentin! Are you making progress with those geography questions?'

Quentin jumped. He had written out the questions Mr Cheeseman set him in his best handwriting, and underlined them neatly, and left small spaces after each one for the answers. He hadn't put any answers.

'Er, sort of . . .'

'Excellent, excellent,' said Mr Cheeseman, and then, 'Ah!'

Outside, a small figure hesitated at the vicarage gate, and then walked towards the house. Quentin recognized her: Miss Dearing, from the terrible tea party. She wore a red flowery summer coat and an orange straw hat over her grey hair. Quentin had never seen an old lady dressed so brightly.

Mr Cheeseman tidied his sermon notes away and said, 'Quentin, please take your Geography questions and finish them in the Snug.' This always happened when the vicar had a visitor he couldn't avoid seeing.

The Snug was very far from snug, being even darker and gloomier than the study. There was space only for the wooden chair and table that Quentin was supposed to work at, and an armchair so hard and lumpy that no one would ever bother slacking off from lessons to stretch out in it. Quentin wished he was doing anything, anything at all, other than Geography. He spread out his work and sighed.

In the cramped and freezing dungeon, John Horsefield stared at the papers in front of him. His captors had written a false confession and wanted him to put his name to it. The guard would be back at nightfall and if he hadn't signed it by then . . .

Quentin heard Mr Cheeseman in the hallway, showing his visitor out. Guiltily he picked up his pen and began to scratch down something—anything—in answer to Question 1, only to find that the ink had dried up. The door to the Snug opened and the vicar looked in.

'What do you think to a breath of fresh air, Quentin? A delightful day outside, and we're missing it. You know what they say—all work and no play makes Jack a dull boy.'

Quentin shoved back his chair and stood up. He pictured a gentle stroll in the sun, returning to lemonade and fresh-baked cake set out on a table on the lawn. He stretched his shoulders and flexed his wrists, glad to be released from book-work.

'That's right, Quentin, get those muscles working.' Mr Cheeseman swung his own right arm round in an ominous fashion. 'Just time before tea for an hour of cricket practice. You can bat first.'

Oh, no! thought Quentin. Suddenly Geography didn't seem the very worst thing in the world.

8 A CONSTABLE CALLS

Ella Otter pressed her ear to the door of her father's study. On the other side a policeman was speaking to the professor 'on important business'—she'd heard that much from the landing before the door was shut.

It wasn't every day that a policeman called—in fact, Ella couldn't remember that it had ever happened before—and she felt quite entitled to know what was going on. Mrs Prebble had shown him in and returned to the back regions of the house as if she couldn't have cared less, but then the housekeeper pretended not to be interested in gossip. Ella felt the opposite. Having no brothers or sisters (her mother died when she was a baby), no other children in the neighbourhood (except, now, The Boy), and a father who always had his head in a book, she had to rely on her own eyes and ears to come up with anything of interest. Now her nose twitched like a bloodhound's. But the door was thick and the voices mumbled. It was hard to make anything out for certain.

The policeman was only Constable James Towner, a very new recruit to the local force. Not so long ago he had been their newspaper boy, and he made so many mistakes—delivering the wrong paper or tearing the whole front page as he pushed it into the letterbox—

46

that Father referred him as Dozy Jim. Now Dozy Jim was a gawky young constable in clumpy boots and a uniform bristling with buttons, but he was here on official business. It must be something serious.

Yet the voices inside sounded quite easy. They might have been chatting about sport—Constable Towner was very keen on cricket—or the hot weather. Then she heard the words, 'calling at every house to warn them'.

Warn them! About what?

Next came, 'suspicious persons . . . mumble mumble . . . you never know,' then something about 'more valuable items going missing'.

Professor Otter laughed. 'I think a burglar would find little of interest in this house, Constable,' he said.

A burglar! There must have been more robberies.

'The things that I have here are not what most people would find valuable,' Professor Otter went on. 'As you can see . . . mumble mumble . . .'

Ella knew exactly what he meant. High Gables was stuffed with things that were very precious to her father—and to Ella—but they weren't polished and expensive-looking. There were old bones and stones her father discovered on his archaeological excavations, and then the dusty books and strange relics he couldn't resist collecting on their trips to second-hand bookshops and antiquaries. They were all around, on shelves and window-sills, in glass-fronted drawers and on table-tops. When the space ran out, books and treasures were piled up on the floor and on every step of the stairs. There was so much clutter that her father would hardly notice if anything vanished, unless it was the paper he was writing on, or the pen in his hand.

The door handle turned. Ella jumped back.

Constable Towner emerged, saying, 'All the same, Sir, if you could keep an eye out for anything unusual. Suspicious characters, that sort of thing.'

'I'll do my best,' Professor Otter told him. But Ella could still hear the laughter in his voice.

'Did you get all that, Ella?' he said, with a wink, as soon as Dozy Jim had gone.

'Um, some of it.'

'You really shouldn't listen at doors, you know. It is very bad manners.'

'It's bad manners not to keep a person informed about things that might affect them.'

'I was intending to inform you—right away—and Mrs Prebble, too. It appears that some light-fingered person is slipping into houses round The Green and stealing things. Constable Towner's calling to tell everyone to keep their eyes open—and their windows shut.'

'Are we going to keep our windows shut?'

'No. It's much too hot. And who would steal this? Or this?' He picked up a yellowing sheep's skull with a strange pattern cut into its bony nose, then a crumbling book whose back cover immediately fell off on to the floor. 'You may keep your eyes open, Ella. I'm sure you will find no end of suspicious characters, but please don't tackle them by yourself!'

'Now you're laughing at me, Father!'

'Not at all.'

'I think it's exciting.'

The professor grunted, 'Storm in a teacup. The major's lost a money clip—without any money in it—and the Finch girls have mislaid a couple of baubles. But talking of observation—how is your Anthropology Scrapbook going?'

'Um . . .'

'I've saved you the latest copy of the Seabourne Herald. You might want to cut out pictures—of country dancing, or the rowing-boat race.'

Ella did not want to cut out pictures of country dancing. Or rowing-boat races. She had no interest in the summer customs of Seabourne. Her studies of a local tribe had concentrated so far only on the new people at Cliffe Lodge. And—with close observation—they were proving quite fascinating.

There had been no more strange meetings in shadowy corners, but when the station van arrived and disgorged a load of luggage, a thin, hatchet-faced woman hopped out, too. She glanced about with a grim expression on her face, as if she didn't think much of The Green, and then set about opening up the house. Later the same day the elegant lady and the motorcar returned. A pink-cheeked housemaid jumped out of the front and was given charge of a tiny, low-slung dog. In the evening Ella spotted the chauffeur riding away on a bicycle. The same bicycle was parked behind the Cliffe Lodge dustbins next morning. She had spied on the elegant lady sitting in the rose arbour (one of her own favourite places) jotting things down in a notebook with a silver pencil. Jazzy music wafted out of windows. Heavenly smells of cooking wafted out of doors. She'd even seen the young housemaid perched on an upturned bucket in a corner of the vegetable patch, and she was writing, too, scribbling in a big red journal. Which was unexpected, to say the least. Ella could almost forgive them for taking over her territory, since there was so much to note in her Anthropology Scrapbook.

At first she was disappointed that were weren't any children in the household—in particular a nice girl or two around her own age—to practise making friends with before school began in earnest. But then they would probably have turned out hopeless, like The Boy, or annoying, like Penny and Popsy Finch, who were almost grown-up and yet still giggled like seven-year-olds. Ella did not have much faith in other children. She'd spent all her time in the company of adults and knew how to get on with them much better than she did with anyone her own age. So it was really just as well that the people at Cliffe Lodge were a perfect sort of study project, something she could really get her teeth into, and did not include someone she might possibly have liked.

As she stood in the hallway with the Seabourne Herald in her hands, Ella realized that her father had already slipped back to his own studies and closed the door. Only Bernard, their big ginger cat, sat in a patch of sunlight, gazing at her as if to say, 'What next?'

9 TROUBLE

NANCY'S JOURNAL

What a day! I got into SO MUCH TROUBLE. But it wasn't ALL my fault.

At the worst point I truly beleeved I was going to get kicked out & I would have to pack my bag & try to get all the way home to London on the train. Even tho I haven't got more than sixpence left in my purse. Mrs Bryce still has not handed over my wages. I knew she wouldn't pay me a bean if she was kicking me out.

But then she drank a STRAWBERRY COCKTAIL straight down & burst out laughing & the Dreadful Moment passed. (This is not the sort of thing that ever happens in Bread Street, I can tell you.)

I am writing this all of a muddle. I must try to be clearer. It was a bad day but I can say I have Gained in Wisdom. Here is what I learned today:

Number 1. TRADESMENS DOOR

Tradesmen are not to call at the front door. But if they do I have to tell them:

That is not the place for deliveries, thank you very much, go round the back!

Then I have to run right through the house—but I mustn't look as if I am running—and answer the back door to the same tradesman. It sounds like a right old waste of my time! Anyhow, it was just a very polite delivery man bringing a neat little package of Mrs Bryce's new Calling Cards—not a great haunch of blood-drenched beef! I don't see what the fuss was about.

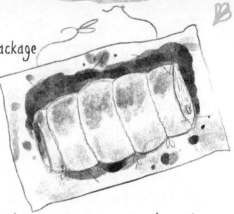

Mrs Bryce only spotted it cos she was coming down the stairs at the time. And—after all that fuss & bother—she seems very pleased with her Calling Cards, which have her new address printed on them.

Number 2. CALLERS

When someone (not a Tradesman) comes to the front door I must get their name & ask them to wait while I see if Mrs Bryce is in. If they give me a Calling Card I must bring it on a tray.

I said, 'But I know if you ARE in, M'm. I don't have to come and see if you are.'

Then Mrs Bryce told me that whether she was in or not was UP TO HER. 'It's a polite convention, Nancy!' she said, all ~~ecksax~~ exasperated. 'I am training you up to be a useful maid-servant. You must listen to me and never answer back. That's the sort of behaviour that gets a girl her marching orders!'

(That was the 1st time I came close to losing my job today.)

It seems a lady can be At Home or not, whatever suits her, even if the caller standing out there in the hallway knows exactly where she is.

'I expect to have a great many visitors—' Mrs Bryce went on—'and you must know the correct way to behave. I might not want to see that particular caller, or I might want to see them but not at present. I might have a headache or feel like taking a nap or I might already be entertaining someone much more fassinating! So I say—and then YOU say, as polite as can be—that I am Not At Home.'

Apparently this is not TELLING A LIE.

I'm sure if someone rang the doorbell and it was me that was putting my feet up in the kitchen it wouldn't be fine to shout 'WE'RE NOT AT HOME!'

(And my poor feet need the rest much more than Mrs Bryce's delicate toes in her rose-pink silk slippers.)

Makes me think of what Grandma says. 'There's one law for the Rich and another for the Poor.'

Even when A POLICEMAN came to the door Mrs Bryce still had to think about whether she wanted to see him & made a great sighing before she let me show him in. I waited by the doorway with the calling card tray (not that he had a calling card, just a great big hat which he balanced on his arm) (his face was very red too) so I could behave in the correct way and still listen in.

His name was Constable Towner and he was calling about some robberies that have taken place around & about. Nothing much stolen & nobody hurt so far as I could make out—Mrs Bryce did not look at all WORRIED—but we are to keep doors and windows locked and not leave valuables in view. Also we should beware of ~~sup~~ Suspishus Persons.

'Have you a ~~discr~~ descripshun?' Mrs Bryce asked as cool as a cucumber but the Policeman said, 'No, just look out for anyone acting odd.' 'And what should we do if we see one?' Mrs Bryce asked. It was almost as if she was having fun with him.

'A capable person could apprehend him,' he said. (It sounded as if he was reciting this bit.) 'But I would advise ladies to try & stay calm, and summon help at once.'

Which is a fat lot of good! What if the help was a long way off? Any burglar would take to his heels while ladies were busy shrieking & fainting. Not that Mrs Bryce strikes me as the Fainting Type.

When I showed him out he stopped to wipe the sweat off his forehead before he put his hat back on. He looked very young for a Policeman. I almost felt sorry for him. (Almost.)

But this visit led to Number 3. The WORST THING that happened today was when I learned:- **DO NOT TRY TO STOP A ROBBER without proper evidence that he is one.**

(No matter how odd he is acting!)

After lunch I went down the garden to throw some peelings out & see if I couldn't find a quiet spot for 5 minutes with my latest book. But what I found instead was someone looking MOST SUSPISHUS. Down the far end where the trees begin to thicken up there was someone—a man—nipping from one bush to the next, taking a peep at the house and then creeping to the next place. I just stood & stared. I couldn't beleve my eyes—not so soon after that Policeman had warned us. He must have come in off the golf course path and he clearly had Cliffe Lodge in mind.

I concluded that he was not a very good burglar, drawing attention to himself by darting about like that. Also he wasn't dressed for concealment. If I was creeping about a garden I'd wear old green tweeds (if I had any). But he was in a noisy blazer with raspberry-red stripes & cream cricket trousers & he had a straw hat in his hand just like a white flag. And a big grin on his face!

I have NO INTENSHUN of Breaking The Law—but I can say that if I was to go burgling I would be a darn sight more clever about it than this.

I remembered the Policeman's words: stay calm and summon help—well, there was only Cook & Mrs Bryce in the house. And the burglar was getting nearer every minute. He'd got to the rose arch by then. From there it was only a quick dash across the lawn and into the open French windows where he might do anything.

A capable person could apprehend him. A capable person indeed did. I jumped out thru that thin bit in the hedge and flung my bowl of peelings at his head. Just at the same moment Mrs Bryce stepped out of the French windows with a look of shock on her face. The burglar yelled 'Surprise!'

55

And it WAS a surprise for the wet peelings hit the side of his face & spilled down his blazer & he rocked on his feet as if he was going to go over.

Mrs Bryce just said 'Darling, what on earth?' & then she saw me and I knew at once that despite my Best Intenshuns I had NOT BEHAVED CORRECTLY yet again.

Mrs Bryce went white with rage and gave me another good scolding for being UTTERLY BRAINLESS (!!) while her visitor just laughed.

(Which made him a Good Sport since he was the one with muddy wet peelings down him.)

He sent me off to fetch a towel & when I came back he had made a pink Cocktail for himself & Mrs Bryce and had got her to laugh about it as well. 'Come on Connie' he said. 'Look on the funny side!'

For how was I to know that a most suspishus character would turn out to be an old friend of the Lady of the House? Mrs Bryce says he will often be dropping in. His name is Mr Gommershall but she called him Gee-Gee. (Which is what Grandma says when she means horse.) (Tho he doesn't look anything like a horse. He is rather handsome, in fact.)

He certainly saved my bacon. Tho if he hadn't been acting so strange I should not have had to APPREHEND HIM in the first place!

I wonder if she is going to become <u>Mrs Gommershall</u> next?

10 MY BURGLAR THEORY

NANCY'S JOURNAL

I am quite worn out after such an eventful day but I just wanted to add another bit. I keep thinking about what that Policeman said.

My Burglar Theory:

No one has seen a Stranger about—because the Burglar is <u>not</u> a stranger!

Whoever is doing it grabs some small fancy thing in passing—like grabbing a cake or sweet without ~~permia~~ permisshun. (Only a real burglar would know what to do next with really valuable stuff like Gold or precious Jewels.)

The weather is hot & everyone's windows have been wide open.

So it does not take much skill.

A child might do it!

In which case there are 2 likely suspects:

A boy around here who acts Very Odd always peering and creeping about. (I know I got that wrong today but that is not THE POINT.)

Also a little girl—a very poor-looking scruffy type—who hangs around Cliffe Lodge & scuttles away thinking I have not spotted her. Well, I HAVE.

It could be either of them. They could be stealing for a dare—or for the money—or just because they are MEAN LOW TYPES.

This is my Theory but I need some evidence to back it up. But I beleeve I have more of a clue who did it than that dopey-looking Policeman.

11 ANTHROPOLOGY

'Got you!'

Ella jumped out of her skin. She had thought her hiding place between the wheelbarrow and the garden shed was perfectly safe. But the housemaid from Cliffe Lodge had somehow crept up behind her—and pounced!

At least it wasn't the grim-faced old Cook who'd found her.

The girl grabbed Ella's shoulder and gave her a shake. 'What are you up to? You've been sneaking around all morning. There's a policeman on the look-out for the likes of you.'

Ella wriggled out of her grasp, stood up, and straightened her glasses. She glared at the girl through their smudged lenses. The maid's cheeks were pinker than usual and gingery hair was fighting its way out from beneath her cap.

'Dozy Jim!?' Ella said, defiantly. 'He isn't looking for me.'

The housemaid grinned at her, unconvinced. 'You're scruffy as a gypsy and always skulking round the dustbins. If you really need scraps to keep you from starving, I could put something aside for you. But if you're after stealing—'

Ella was horrified. 'That's very kind of you, but I'm certainly not starving. And I'm not stealing. As a matter of fact I'm—'

But she couldn't say what she was doing. She couldn't say, 'Actually, I'm studying your household as if you were a rare Amazon tribe. I've peered through windows, and noted your tidy kitchen, and your perfectly-stocked pantry, and the cook's cracked old boots standing next to her bed. I've watched your mistress come and go in her motor car, and I've followed you at a distance when you take the dog for his walk. I've seen you eat half the strawberries when Cook sends you out to pick a bowlful, and I know you read sixpenny thrillers in your moments off. And you chew the end of your pencil when you write!'

Instead she said, 'I live next door and I—I'm used to coming into this garden. That's all.' It sounded rather feeble. 'I'm Eleanor Mary Otter. Professor Otter's daughter. The eminent archaeologist.'

'And I'm the Maharajah of Timbuktu,' the housemaid said. But at least she was still grinning.

'I really am. Why won't you believe me?'

The girl shrugged. ''Cos your spectacles are mended with a lump of glue. 'Cos somebody needs to sew up your jumper.' She pointed to Ella's grubby sleeve, which was coming unravelled at the seam. ''Cos I don't think professors' daughters look like they slept in a ditch.'

'Huh! That just shows how little you know. Professors' daughters don't care a fig about appearances—and neither do professors!'

It did cross Ella's mind that she didn't know any other professors' daughters—but she had met other professors, and none of them looked as if they ever glanced in a mirror. Her father never noticed how she dressed, and Mrs Prebble had long ago given up trying to keep Ella tidy. But to say that she was scruffy and imply that she was a beggar . . .

'I'm doing a study,' she went on, feeling bolder now. 'I'm studying Anthropology and that means observing people's behaviour. I can't do that if I stay in my own house and garden. The only people there are my father and Mrs Prebble and Bernard our cat.'

'So Anthro-pop-logy is the art of being nosey, is it?'

'No. Not exactly. Not quite.' Ella twitched at her fringe again, and tucked the stray end of wool from her jumper sleeve back inside her cuff. 'It's purely scientific. And what I've observed about you is that you sneak off down the garden to read a book when you should probably be polishing the silver or—or dusting things.'

'It's none of your business what I do in my spare time.'

Ella realized that she had struck the wrong note. She coughed importantly like the vicar did at the beginning of his sermon, and said, in a very serious voice, 'But it's the business of Anthropology. Besides, I'm glad you like reading. I love reading. Our house is full of books. I don't suppose I'd get to the end of them if I read every minute of every day for a whole year!'

The girl was staring at her now, no longer smiling. Perhaps she had gone on a bit. But she couldn't help adding, 'I've seen you writing, too, in that big red notebook of yours.'

'Oh, have you now?'

'Yes. I did wonder what it was you were writing.'

'Maybe I'm doing a study, too,' the girl said. 'Maybe I'm studying all the sneaky little kids that creep round The Green, poking their noses where they shouldn't. What if that's what I was writing?'

'Um,' said Ella, taking a step backwards and finding herself pressed up against the shed. 'That would be very interesting.'

'Maybe I'm studying those burglaries that policeman told us about, and who's most likely to have done them.'

Ella stepped sideways, towards the hedge. 'I'd probably better go now. I expect Mrs Prebble wants me back for lunch.' One more step and she'd be in the gap between the privet bushes and almost on home ground. 'You're very wrong if you think the burglar's *me*, you know. Your reasoning is utterly misplaced.'

The girl was frowning like thunder now.

I've made a complete hash of this, Ella thought, and ducked away into her own garden. Bernard was sitting in the middle of the pathway, and gave her a look as if to say, Yes, you have.

Lunch was sardine salad, eaten on her own at the kitchen table. Ella cut her bread-and-butter into strips and nibbled each one carefully, end to end. She was busy thinking. If the maidservant at Cliffe Lodge was really making a study of the burglaries, Ella might be able to offer assistance. They had got off on the wrong foot, but perhaps if she started again—with some helpful suggestions—then all was not lost. After all, she knew the area well and the people at Cliffe Lodge were strangers to The Green.

Helping solve a mystery—and beating Dozy Jim to the solution—would be a perfect holiday project. It might even count as Anthropology.

'You again,' the girl said. She shut her red notebook sharply and gripped its cover with both hands.

Ella had to admit that this wasn't the best start. But she smiled and pointed at the notebook. 'Yes, me again! Listen. I've been thinking. If you really are studying the robberies I could help you. For instance, I could question everyone who's been burgled. I'm sure they won't mind if they know it's for my Anthropological studies. I mean, if that's what you're really writing . . .' The smile faded and she bit her lip. 'Also, I've come up with a theory. Do you know what a theory is?'

'Course I do!'

'Good. I—er—only meant that not everybody does. My theory is that a housemaid is a Very Important Person.'

'How d'you make that out?'

'Because the housemaid is the one person who knows everything that goes on in a house. The cook spends all her time in the kitchen, whereas a housemaid goes everywhere and keeps an eye on everything. It's your job to do so. You open the door to all the visitors, and ask who they are, and notice when they leave.'

The girl was definitely looking interested now.

Ella rushed on, 'And, you see, because you do things like dusting and polishing, you're familiar with what's there—every last paperweight and silver salt-pot—so you'd know if anything disappeared. But you'd also know if it had just rolled under a table or slipped down the side of the sofa, because you're the one who has to tidy up.'

'So . . . what are you saying?'

'I mean that a housemaid is the perfect person to tell if a crime is committed!'

'Hmm. I'm new at this job, and still learning,' the girl said. 'I mustn't do anything that might upset the Missus. And Mrs Bryce is easy to upset, I can tell you.'

Ella glanced around. The garden was still and the house perfectly quiet. There was no one who might overhear them. 'I'm not asking you to do anything,' she hissed, 'I'm just saying, should anything happen, that you as the housemaid are perfectly placed to look into it. You're a sort of Sherlock Holmes in apron and lace cap!'

'A what?'

'Sherlock Holmes. He's a very clever detective. In a book.'

The housemaid clutched her own book to her chest and stood up. 'I ought to go in now. All that dusting and polishing, and nobody else to do it!'

'Wait! What's your name? I told you mine.'

'Nancy. Nancy Parker.'

Ella stuck out her hand. The girl looked surprised, tucked her notebook beneath her elbow, and reluctantly took the offered hand.

'Pleased to meet you, Nancy Parker! Most people call me Ella. Um, I could lend you one of my Sherlock Holmes stories, if you like?'

Nancy looked even more surprised. 'I'd rather have a dictionary. Got one of them, have you?'

'Heaps. What language d'you want it in?'

Nancy frowned. 'What language? Are you nuts? English, of course!'

Ella watched her go off down the garden path. She couldn't decide whether she had made a good impression on Nancy or not. People were strange—even when you had been studying them for ages.

12 FOOD FOR THOUGHT

NANCY'S JOURNAL

Due to information recently receeved I've had to alter my Burglar Theory:—

The scruffy little Beggar Girl is not a gypsy—or a beggar—at all. Her name is Elenor Otter. She lives next door & her father is a well-known Porfesor. (So she says.)

EVIDENCE FOR

1. She does speak nicely (now I have heard her speak.)
2. On closer inspecktion her clothes look Well Made and good ~~ewal~~ quality stuff.
3. She must be one of those kids that cannot keep anything clean for a minute.
4. Porfesser types do not care how they look. (I only have Ella's own word for this.)

EVIDENCE AGAINST

1. I only have her word for <u>all</u> of this.
2. Except I did see her slip into the next-door house (High Gables it is called).
She could just be scrounging round there too.
3. Her glasses look like this:—

Would an EDUCATED PERSON let his child wear such things??
(I think No. 2 is actually EVIDENCE FOR.)
So that leaves just the boy as a

LATER ON

I was just putting all this down when that Ella Otter popped up again right under my nose. What cheek! (Tho I don't think she saw what I was writing.)

She acts pretty strange—but not everything she says is nonsense. She's got a Theory about HOUSEMAIDS!! According to her I am perfectly placed to see all that goes on: — I am a Detective in an apron and cap. She thinks I'm trying to find the burglar & wants to help me do it.

This is certainly FOOD FOR THOGHT.

13 LOOKING FOR A CONNECTION

Even though Nancy Parker hadn't said yes, Ella was determined to be of assistance. From Mrs Prebble she found out the names of everyone who had been burgled, and then she called on them. She made notes in her Anthropology Scrapbook, dividing a double page into four columns. One was headed 'People', the next 'Houses', and the third one 'Things'. She noted down the name of the person, their address, and the item that had gone missing. The last column simply had a '?' at the top. It was empty. She was looking for some sort of connection, but hadn't come up with anything yet.

She had just visited the last person on her list—Miss La Roche. Miss La Roche lived at one end of Apple Cottage, Miss Dearing at the other. Miss La Roche's small garden was neat, while Miss Dearing's large one was a mess. Chickens scratched holes and made dust-baths, ducks and geese paddled the grass into mud, and Pancho the donkey nibbled at everything he could reach, including laundry hanging out to dry. Pancho used to give children rides on the beach; Miss Dearing felt he was too old for such work and rescued him. But she could never rid him of his bad habits.

Miss La Roche reported only one thing taken: 'A silver thimble that belonged to my beloved grand-mère. It was the first of the hot days, and I had all the windows thrown wide. My sewing bag was on the table in my sitting room, open because I was in the middle of some needlepoint. When I looked for my thimble that evening—it was gone! Nothing was disturbed. He's a sly one, that thief. He came in and out as quietly as a cat.'

Sitting on the grassy bank outside Apple Cottage, Ella made careful notes. In the column headed '?' she wrote 'Cat burglar?' A voice interrupted her.

'Ella, dear! What are you up to?'

Ella plastered a polite smile on her face and looked up. Miss Dearing was leaning over her garden gate. The two neighbours were determinedly nosey. If one had a visitor, the other had to know all about it.

'I've just been asking Miss La Roche about her robbery.'

Miss Dearing's eyebrows crumpled and her eyes filled with tears.

'Oh, I didn't mean to worry you!' Ella rushed over to Miss Dearing and tried to pat her hand. But Miss Dearing fended her off.

'Worried? I'm not worried! Not about burglars. My geese are better than any guard dog!'

'So you haven't found anything missing, then?' Ella checked, just to make sure. Dozy Jim could easily have missed someone out. Miss Dearing, who hadn't been burgled, seemed more upset than Miss La Roche, who had.

'Found? Missing? Me? No!' Miss Dearing still looked extremely flustered. Then the donkey started up a loud heehawing from behind the hedge and she darted away to see what was the matter.

Ella headed home, lost in thought. As she walked past the vicarage garden, she heard the sound of thumping feet and then a ball striking something hard. When she went to school next term she would have to do Games. It was not a pastime she had much—in fact, any—experience of.

There was another thump, followed by a cry of pain.

'Oh, bad luck, Quentin!' she heard Mr Cheeseman call.

14 MY THEORY ABOUT COOK

NANCY'S JOURNAL

I've got a new hiding place for this Journal! I found a loose floorboard under my bed when I was sweeping so I'm sticking it underneath. I don't trust leaving it in my drawer—not now I'm working on my Theory about Cook.

I've been thinking a lot about what that kid Ella said—about a Housemaid being a <u>Very</u> Important Person in an investigation. (Not where the police are concerned. Constable Towner did not want to speak to me.) If a crime DID take place here I may well spot clues the Police would miss.

But I think that ~~EMBRASS~~ EMBARASSMENT with Mr Gommershall has put me off the whole burglar business for now. Having A Theory about it is <u>one</u> thing. Being the one to actually catch the criminal is <u>quite</u> another.

(I don't suppose Mrs Bryce would care if something was stolen anyway. The house was let furnished so none of the ornaments are hers—just a few photos she brought with her.)

And since a Policeman's been round warning everyone, it's probably enuff to scare ~~that boy~~ the burglar off.

So instead I am working on my Theory about Cook. I have had a bad feeling about her from the start. Mrs

Bryce may trust her—but I don't.

I shall write down the cause of my SUSPISHUNS—then I can add anything new that I see. (Or hear.) This Journal will be a Diary of Detection!

I'm convinced Cook's got A PAST & I reckon it's a dark one. My reasons why:-

- She never talks about it.
- She never talks at all if she can help it. (Except when Alfred butters her up.)
- She is called Mrs Jones—but where is Mr Jones?
- She could be hiding behind a false name. Jones is the most common English name there is. (Except for Smith.) People call themselves Smith when they wish to be anonymous. Mrs Jones might be EVEN MORE CUNNING than that.
- She doesn't like husbands at all. Is what happened in the Past to do with them?*
- She does not look like a cook in my opinion. I can't help feeling that Cooks should be plump. Mrs Jones is as bony & stringy as a worn-out horse. Perhaps she has not been a cook for long enuff to get plump.

 VS

72

- So what was she BEFORE? (In her Dark Past.)
- However it's true she is a very good cook so she must have had lots of practiss.
- She stays with Mrs Bryce when she could get a much better job.
- Is this becos Mrs Bryce knows her dark secret? Does that mean Mrs B. has A HOLD over her?
- Or does Cook have some kind of hold over Mrs B.?? (What?)

   * Why I think this is true:-

When Alfred (and the cooking sherry) got her talking, she clammed right up when it came to talk of Mr Treadgold— Mrs Bryce's 1st (?) husband. She never menshuns the 2nd husband at all. Not even to say God Rest His Soul. Yet he must have been her employer when he was alive & married to Mrs Bryce. The reason may be that Mr Bryce was not a pleasant man. (This is mere speculation.) But my experiense is that Cook is not a pleasant woman. (Not speculation.)

   So there it is:—

A Good Investigation requires Good Clear Thinking and Good Clear Notes.

(Nancy Parker's Theory of Detection No. 1)

15 PSYCHOLOGY

Ella Otter knew exactly when Nancy walked the little dog every morning and what route she took. She slipped out of her own house early and laid a line of white beach pebbles along the front path of Cliffe Lodge. She added a pair of twigs to form

then hid in the big hydrangea bush by the gate.

'Did you like it?' she asked, jumping out and startling the dog.

'Was that *your* sign?' Nancy asked.

'Of course! It's an excellent way to signal to you, don't you think? Secret, too.'

Nancy looked from left to right and crossed the road, the dog trotting beside her. 'How is it secret if you jump out like that in front of people?'

The milkman was driving past and waved from the seat of his cart. Even the milkman's horse gave the pair of them a curious look.

Ella ignored them and trailed Nancy along the edge of The Green. The dog hurried, pausing only to sniff at odd clumps of grass. Ella had to trot to keep up with them. It was astonishing how fast a dog with such minuscule legs could go.

'I wanted to show you my notes,' she said. 'I've made a list of everything that's been stolen. I thought you might know about—about things . . .'

Nancy grinned. 'Because it's my job to dust and polish 'em?'

'Because of my Theory—remember? How a housemaid sees what goes on and how people behave, in public and in private. You must know a lot about psychology.'

'About sigh-what?'

'Psychology.'

'This is another one of your Ologies, is it?'

'Psychology means the inner workings of the psyche. The mind. Why people do things and what it all means. A man called Dr Freud sort of—invented it—and everyone in brain-doctor circles is talking about it.'

Ella wasn't sure that she had explained it very well. She wasn't sure that she understood it very well. Father had told her all about it. But quite often he talked to her as if she was a grown-up, even a professor like himself, instead of a child of eleven.

They had reached the lychgate to the church and stopped beneath its roof. Ella said, 'Here, read the list for yourself. I brought you a dictionary, too. You said you wanted one. And a Sherlock Holmes. I left them under the hydrangea bush.'

'Is that a bribe?'

Ella felt her cheeks colour up. 'No. Most certainly not.'

Nancy cast her eye over the items in Ella's notebook. 'Everything's small.'

'Yes! Even Dozy—er, Constable Towner—noticed that.'

'Everything's something that needs a good polish.'

'Valuable, in other words.'

'Everything's glittery or shiny. Eye-catching.'

'I thought that, too. Because sometimes people had things that seem more valuable—to me anyway—and they weren't taken.'

Nancy fixed her with a calculating look. 'How do you know?'

'Because I visited everyone on this list and interviewed them myself. Not only interviewed them, but observed their surroundings, too. A good investigation relies on good observation. Sherlock Holmes was stunningly good at observation!'

Ella took back her Anthropology Scrapbook and turned the page. 'Look. I've drawn a map of The Green and the lanes leading off it. Every house the burglar has been to, and I've numbered them in the order he—or she—took. The only ones not visited so far are High Gables and Cliffe Lodge. I've put a question-mark over the vicarage. Mrs Cheeseman claims one of her best tea-spoons went missing after she'd set out tea on a table on the lawn. But I think she's just mislaid it. Who would pinch a single spoon?'

Nancy studied the scrapbook in silence. Ella was disappointed. She was proud of her efforts, and felt sure that even Father would approve of her note-taking and map-making skills. In the end she felt forced to ask, 'What do you think?'

Nancy looked thoughtful. 'Whoever he is, this thief's got a magpie eye,' she said.

'We can't assume it's a "he". We mustn't jump to conclusions.'

'You're right. He, she, or it,' said Nancy cheerfully. 'Sorry, I can't stand here chatting all day. Mrs Bryce's breakfast won't get up those stairs by itself.'

Ella watched her go, the dog at her heels. She'd made a hash of it again. 'Bye . . . Don't forget to pick up the books,' she called out. Nancy raised a hand—it might have been to say thanks or to say goodbye—but she didn't turn round.

16 GOOD AND BAD

NANCY'S JOURNAL

I'm starting to have some regrets about the Biscuit
Factory. I remember Aunty Bee said that during the
War lots of girls gave up jobs in service to work in the
factories that made shells for the guns. They got better
pay & went home every night. Even if they worked long
hours the rest of the time was theirs. No running to
answer every bell or waiting up after midnight for the
Missus to come home from a party. A factory job was a
Great Improvement & once they got a taste for it no one
wanted to go back into service.

(Perhaps I am just feeling HOMESICK.)

So I am going to ~~wai~~ way up the Good and the Bad
Things about this job.

Good:-

1st. Even tho I work hard—it COULD BE WORSE. Mrs
Bryce is out a lot & Cook slides off to her room after lunch
for a nap. I still squeeze in time to write this Journal—I
can look up spellings in Ella's Dictionary now—and read my
books. (I had a glance at that Sherlock Holmes Mystery
Ella lent me—lots & lots of pages of v. thin paper like in
a Bible & the writing is tiny. Perhaps I shall get round to
it one day. Right now I'm gripped by 'Scream Blue Murder'
where a man goes round marrying rich widows & then
bumps them off for their money. At least that's who you

think is doing it. But there may be another twist.)

2nd. THE SEASIDE. Like Aunty Bee said—I could be somewhere dull & dreary. Here I can see the sea from my bedroom window (just about.)

So that is the 3rd— MY ROOM.

4th THE FOOD. Delicious. Things I never ate in all my life! Things I never heard of!! Now I have tasted good cooking I know that Gran's food was even worse than we thought. (I feel v. guilty putting that.)

Bad:-

1st: Still NO WAGES. I asked Alfred if he's had any yet & he told me that him & the car come together. Mrs Bryce hires them both from his uncle's garage by the day. She pays his uncle & his uncle pays him. I don't dare ask Cook! She'd bite my head off & put it in a clear jelly & serve it up for dinner.

So COOK is the 2nd bad thing. If only she was nice & kind instead of irritable & snappy. Is it because her dark past is playing on her conscience??

3rd: BEING SO FAR FROM HOME. Tho I suppose there's always letters.

4th: BEING LONELY. Having Alfred here has cheered things up a lot. And that funny kid Ella from next door with her Theory and her Oll-o-gies. They stop me thinking too much about home.

(I ought to put ALFRED and ELLA in the list under Good Things.)

Then there's the thing I'm not sure about—if it is Good or Bad. I will put it in the category of Interesting. I mean my investigation of Cook.

LATER

Just a quick thoght: another Observation. Cook may have no time for HUSBANDS but she has a soft spot for Alfred & fawns on Mr Gommershall. She is always quick to find all the silly things he asks for when he visits—like chipped ice for cocktails—or toasted cheese in the middle of the afternoon! Yet she dislikes girls—or at any rate housemaids—or is it just ME?

I shall have to ask Ella. It is probably something to do with Sye-collar-gee. (I can't find that word in the Dictionary.)

17 DISCOVERIES

NANCY'S JOURNAL

I have been in Cook's room!! Everyone was out & I couldn't resist having a quick peep.

It was not entirely <u>sneaky</u> because you could say it's my job to clean in there. Except Cook doesn't want me to & says she will take care of it herself. Which is SUSPICIOUS! (I know how to spell that word now cos I looked it up.)

There wasn't much to see. Can this be all she owns? If this is all she's got it is rather sad. It's my belief she keeps her other stuff somewhere else, just like half my things are in my bedroom back home. I wonder if Cook's got any family and—if so—where they live? Even someone as miserable as Cook must have had a family once. They may ALL BE DEAD by now which is very sad indeed. (If they are that may explain why she is so miserable.) I fetch the post every morning & Cook has never had any letters. Not since I've been working here.

CONTENTS OF COOK'S ROOM

(apart from clothes & shoes) (& furniture of course):—
<u>Beside the bed</u>
* Small photo in cardboard frame—woman in old-fashioned clothes with a small child in a lacy frock on her knee. (If Cook has a grim face, this woman is twice as bad. Must run in the family!)
* A book of Illnesses and Remedies—well-thumbed.
* A Bible—not well-thumbed.

* Several newspapers Cook has not thrown out yet—all the headlines about MURDER or DEATH of one kind or another. She always turns to these kind of stories in the paper—she takes a great interest in people who have come to a GRUESOME END!

On the chest of drawers
* Green glass bowl of hairpins and hatpins—the latter very long & sharp.
* Tin box with small brown glass bottles in.

Under the bed
* A suitcase (unlocked)
* with a coat in it (folded)
* beneath that a big envelope. At first I thoght this held letters but then I saw they were newspaper cuttings—some old & yellow. From what I could see they were mostly Births & Marriages & DEATHS.

Not much time to examine them—or anything else—as I heard the motor-car in the drive. I had to put everything back just as I found it & get out quick. As I was going I noticed a newspaper clipping on the floor so I snatched it up and stuck it in my apron pocket.

My heart was thumping like the big drum in the Sally Army band. I was sure MY GUILT would be written all over my face for everyone to see but I had an idea. I took the long feather duster & rushed off in search of cobwebs so if I appeared flustered I could say a Spider had just fallen down my neck.

> It is a poor show for a Detective to look **GUILTY** when Investigating. Crimes must be solved!
>
> (Nancy Parker's Theory of Detection No. 2)

Questions:

<u>What</u> is in those bottles? Medicines? (Some of the Remedies from that book of Illnesses & Remedies?) Or could they be POISONOUS LICKWIDS to actually make people ill??

<u>Who</u> is in the photograph? The mystery woman & Cook look alike. It could be her mother. The little child could be Cook as an infant on her mother's lap.

<u>Who</u> are the newspaper cuttings about? People who are connected to Cook? Or people who have met GRUESOME ENDS? Or both??

I've scribbled this down very fast but now I must go & take Mrs Bryce her supper tray. She has stayed in this evening—for once. But I shall not stop THINKING. And keeping a v. close eye on Cook.

P.S. I cannot make head nor tail of that Newspaper Cutting I picked up. I am saving it in here anyway.

Miss Mary Constance Dyer, aged 20, appeared in court on 12th May, charged with Deception. Miss Dyer, who worked as a companion to Mrs Lewis Colton, of Ravenscroft Road, London S.W., is said to have persuaded her employer to part with sums of money for items which Miss Dyer never in fact bought. Miss Dyer then kept the money herself. The charge was brought by Mrs Colton's son.

However, Mrs Colton herself said that Miss Dyer was of good character, came from a respectable family and had recently lost her father. She understood that under distressing circumstances Miss Dyer had made genuine mistakes, and wished the charge to be withdrawn. Magistrates agreed.

18 NOT TOO EXTREME

NANCY'S JOURNAL

I've stolen a moment after breakfast just to write down One Thing. The book I'm reading now—'A Taste For Killing'—put it in my mind but I am sure it is not TOO EXTREME a Theory. Because the more I think about it the more it makes sense.

Cook hates husbands and gets rid of them by MURDEROUS MEANS!

Maybe she started with Mr Jones.

Then she killed Mrs Bryce's first husband (Mr Treadgold) and then Mr Bryce. (If he didn't die in the War, that is.)

She is VERY VERY LOYAL to her employer so if the husbands are no good she takes it into her own hands to deal with them.

I wonder if she bumped off Mr Bryce to make way for Mr Gommershall to marry Mrs B.—Cook is certainly partial to him.

I am convinced the method she used was POISON. (Kept in those brown bottles in her room.) (Or lickwids that if mixed together make a POISON.) It is the perfect way for a cook to kill someone. They could disguise the POISON in a tasty meal. Cook knows so much about food & cooking that it would be easy for her come up with something.

(In 'A Taste for Killing' someone buys weedkiller—he

says it's for the daisies in his lawn—and puts it in his enemies tea!)

All I need now is some <u>PROOF</u>.

But I must get back to work. I'm supposed to scrub the bathroom taps with Sillwood's Paste which makes my hands go red & my fingers burn for ages afterwards.

Oh—I just had to add—I wonder if Mrs Bryce KNOWS? (That her husbands were dead of poisoning!)

(Now I am definitely going.)

19 COMMUNICATION

There had been no more robberies. Ella carried her Anthropology Scrapbook around with her but hadn't added anything to it. No one unfamiliar lurked about. It was the same old neighbours, delivery vans, Miss Dearing rattling about in her donkey cart, Mrs Bryce sweeping past with her chauffeur and her little dog. She was beginning to think that the burglar must be someone from around The Green—someone in the tribe she was studying—that the answer was here right under her nose. But why would anyone here steal from their neighbours? As a tribe they were all quite well-off; they didn't have to dig up grubs to eat or dress themselves in leaves.

Ella took herself into the churchyard and sat on her favourite tomb. It was just the right height, and their names had been worn off by time and the weather so she didn't feel that she was bothering anyone. She got out her notebook, bent it open at the map, and stared at it in the hope that it would give up some unforeseen clue.

Something scrabbled above her. A rain of dusty bark scraps twirled down, landing on her map. A squirrel, probably, or a bird. She tipped back her head to look up.

It was The Boy. Unmistakably, The Boy. Even though it was the holidays he always wore school uniform: grey shirt and shorts and thick grey socks. His face, distorted by the odd angle, peered down between his knees.

'You look hot,' Ella said.

She had meant to say, 'What are you doing here? This is *my* churchyard!'

But he did look hot, puce and sticky and sweaty, and those were the words that popped out of her mouth. Besides, strictly speaking, the churchyard belonged to the church, and the church belonged to the Vicar, and the Vicar was tutor to The Boy. So he probably had more right to think of it as his territory than she did.

'I *am* hot,' he said crossly. 'What's it to you?'

'Just an observation.' Ella snapped her book shut, as he had a bird's-eye view of the map from where he sat. 'What are you doing up there?'

'Just observing,' The Boy said tartly.

Ella answered tartly back. 'Not sneaking about, or anything? Not up in a tree so that you can spy on people?'

There was only silence in reply. Another shower of tree-bark came tumbling down.

'On people going about their innocent business . . .' she added, just to goad him. Of course he was up to something. It was just that she wasn't completely sure what that something was.

'Innocent?' The Boy said, in a funny voice. 'What's innocent got to do with it?'

Ella twisted round so that she could see him better. 'Was it you who lost one of Mrs Cheeseman's silver teaspoons? I bet you were digging in the flowerbed with it, burying one of her rock buns.'

'Rock buns! Why would I bury a rock bun? Mrs Cheeseman's cakes are all right.'

'My tooth came out the last time I tried to eat one,' Ella said.

This remark was met with silence.

'You go to school, don't you? Boarding school, I heard.'

Another silence. This one felt hot and heavy, a resentful withdrawing.

I'm getting good at this psychology business, Ella thought. She tried some more. 'I bet you don't like school. I bet you don't like having to do lessons in your summer holidays, either.'

'What's it to you?' The Boy repeated.

Ella shrugged theatrically, hoping he was still watching. 'Just an observation.'

After a pause, his voice drifted down again. 'Here's another observation . . . You were looking at a map just now. A hand-drawn map. I bet you made it.'

Ella's lips crimped in annoyance. She was the one doing the Psychology. 'What if I did?'

'Just wondering. You didn't want me to see it. Can't be innocent business if you don't want anyone to see.'

'I can make a map if I want without some nosey parker watching me from up a tree! If you must know, it's a summer holiday project my Father set me.'

There was a furious scraping and scrabbling and The Boy landed, dishevelled, on the ground. 'Just wondered,' he said, straightening his shirt and then his glasses, 'why you'd draw a map with certain houses marked, and a dotted line joining them up, and numbers and arrows and things?'

Goodness, Ella thought, does he actually need those glasses?

'You know, you do awfully look hot,' she said. 'Your face is very red. I can't think why you're wearing that thick school shirt—in such warm weather, too.'

The Boy turned even redder. 'It's because it's all I've got to put on. My stupid parents have gone on stupid holiday themselves, and they never bothered to send my summer things on here. They've just tootled off abroad and keep sending me postcards saying how lovely it is. Lovely for them, all right! I'm just about boiling to death!'

Ella felt a twinge of sympathy for him. 'Couldn't Mrs Cheeseman help you out? She keeps a box of clothes in the vestry—all sorts of things. She's always collecting for the next church jumble sale.'

'Jumble sale clothes?!'

Ella looked The Boy up and down. Rumpled and crumpled and stuck about with broken twigs, he was hardly in a position to complain. Besides, she had no difficulty with jumble sale clothes herself. 'You might go and see what there is . . .' she began.

But before anyone could move, the side door of the church opened. It was the entrance nearest the vicarage and was never locked in the daytime. Normally the only person who used it was the Vicar. But instead of Mr Cheeseman, Miss Dearing stepped out. She blinked when she saw Quentin and Ella.

'I just popped into the church for a moment of prayer. So calming,' she explained, with a nervous laugh. 'Ella, dear, I'm going to have to drag you away from your little friend.'

Quentin and Ella both pulled hideous faces at this description.

Miss Dearing appeared not to notice and carried on. 'I need you to run an errand for me. A most urgent one.'

She took Ella by the arm. Her grip was fierce—and unarguable.

'So sorry. Goodbye, young man!'

Ella gave Quentin one quick glance over her shoulder as she was hauled away. She had no idea what her glance was supposed to convey, and Quentin had no idea what to read into it. But it was a glance. A communication.

20 MARIUS

Miss Dearing's half of Apple Cottage was cool and dark. Ella had not been inside it for at least a year, not since Miss Dearing had asked her in to see a baby robin she had rescued. She was feeding it on minced-up worms until it was strong enough to fly. Miss Dearing was a great animal lover and very soft-hearted. (Except when it came to worms.)

Ella had no idea what Miss Dearing wanted her for, unless it was to tell her that she had now been burgled.

'Is it about the—?' she began, but Miss Dearing raised both hands to hush her. Without a word she beckoned Ella into the next room. On a table by the window a bird hopped about in a cage. It certainly wasn't a robin. This bird had gleaming black feathers, with a flash of white and sky-blue on its wing. Its legs were long and strong, and so was its beak. It fixed her with a sharp eye.

'Now,' said Miss Dearing, standing in the middle of the room and twisting her hands together, 'you visited Miss La Roche recently to discuss the robberies, didn't you? I believe you had a map.'

Ella patted her pockets to make sure her precious notebook was still there.

Miss Dearing went on, 'A map of all the houses that

have been burgled along with a note of all the items that went missing.'

Ella nodded enthusiastically. 'Have you found something missing now, Miss Dearing?'

'Missing? Me? Oh dear, no. Quite the opposite.' She twisted her fingers so hard that her knuckles cracked.

The bird raked the bars of his cage with his fierce-looking beak. He put his head on one side and gave Ella what she could only think of as an amused stare.

Miss Dearing seemed to be distracted by the bird. 'You haven't met Marius yet, have you?'

'No. You used to have a robin.'

'Yes! The dear little thing grew up and flew away. Then I came across Marius, with an injured wing.'

As if he knew his name, Marius bounced rapidly along his perch and back again.

'Marius is a great character!' said Miss Dearing. 'Corvids—that is the crow family—are very intelligent. But that cage really is too small for him.'

'Is he recovered now? Can't you let him out?'

'Oh . . .' groaned Miss Dearing. 'That's exactly what I did. I decided it was time to help him learn to live in the outside world again. I opened the window and left it up to him. At first he just hopped outside and hopped back in. But soon he began to take short flights.'

Ella nodded some more. She wanted to look encouraging. Miss Dearing seemed rather sad about Marius's recovery.

'And he then brought something back with him. It was a shiny penny. I thought he was so clever! Next came a bit of glass. Then a button in mother-of-pearl.'

Ella saw that Marius had the lid of a syrup tin propped

up like a mirror in the corner of the cage. As if to show that he was enjoying this story about himself, he hopped over and tapped it with his beak.

Miss Dearing sighed. She went to the sideboard, opened a drawer and brought something out. It was a drawstring cotton bag, with a pattern of yellow rosebuds on it. Mrs Prebble had made Ella something similar, to keep her party shoes in.

Miss Dearing carried the bag over to Marius's table as if it was full of rocks. She loosened the string and let it fall open. Ella peered inside: shiny things. Familiar things. She counted a money clip, a signet ring, a silver-plated spoon, a sparkly brooch . . .

'Did Marius take these?'

Miss Dearing nodded.

'Then there isn't a robber on the loose? At least, not a human one?'

Miss Dearing's eyes glinted with tears. 'It's in a magpie's nature to pick up shiny things. He doesn't know he's stealing.'

Ella tried to reassure her. 'I suppose they usually pick up the sort of things Marius began with—dropped coins, lost buttons, broken glass.'

'Yes, but then he grew very bold! He must have gone into people's houses. He developed a taste for it.'

'Through their open windows! Miss La Roche said she left her windows wide and her sewing bag was nearby.' Ella was overjoyed at finding the solution. Just wait until Dozy Jim heard all about it! 'Constable Towner—'

Miss Dearing clutched the bag of stolen goods with one hand and Ella's arm with the other. 'No! Constable Towner must know nothing!'

'But—'

'No buts, Ella Otter!'

Ella was shocked at how fiercely Miss Dearing could glare at a person! Her eyes were quite as sharp and as wild as the bird's. Beside her, Marius leapt violently to and fro in his cage.

'Other people will not be as understanding about Marius as you have been,' Miss Dearing said. Her voice shook. 'Other people may want rid of a thieving magpie. I can't let that happen. Marius is innocent—he cannot help his nature. We must not blame him.'

'No, of course not,' Ella agreed. Her arm felt quite sore. Miss Dearing was much stronger than she looked.

'So you must return all these things!' Miss Dearing thrust the bag at Ella.

'Me?'

'You know where they have come from. You know who they belong to. I have no idea. These things just appeared in my sitting room as if by magic.'

'But I—I couldn't possibly—'

'You said yourself you made the map!'

'Yes, I did. But—what if—?'

'What if what? Do it with utmost secrecy. No one must be able to hold Marius to blame.'

Miss Dearing clearly didn't have a detective's mind. Even Dozy Jim could probably see the weakness in her plan.

'What if I'm caught putting them back? They'll hold *me* to blame!'

'They won't blame you. How could they? You're Ella Otter, daughter of the respected professor.'

This didn't seem like much of an argument to Ella.

She opened her mouth to say so, when a familiar voice sounded from outside.

'Coo-ee!'

'Drat, that's Violette. Go, Ella. Save Marius for me.' Miss Dearing pushed Ella from the room, put her own head out of the window and trilled in a quite different tone, 'What can I do for you, Miss La Roche?'

Ella hurried away with her bag of stolen goods. She didn't know whether to swing it nonchalantly from one wrist—except that it would jingle!—or clutch it to her chest and huddle over it—except that would look as if she had something to hide!

It was so unfair. She'd only been trying to help everyone by solving the crimes, and now Miss Dearing had forced this impossible task on her. If she took the bag home Mrs Prebble was sure to discover it. Despite the untidiness of the Otters' house, she had an infallible ability to know where things were—and to spot something new. Ella sighed. She felt like chucking the bag of stolen goods over a hedge and forgetting all about it.

Which suddenly struck her as a very good idea. And there, right to hand, was the perfect place. Tall, thick, evil-smelling, its slippery green leaves all splattered with lurid yellow—the vicarage hedge!

Ella dropped to the ground and pretended to retie her shoelace. In a flash she stuffed the bag under a tangle of branches, and then pushed it further in, just to be sure. If she could work out a way to do it without incriminating herself, she might even point Dozy Jim towards it and let him think he had solved the crime all by himself.

She got up again, brushed at her skirt and sauntered off, feeling strangely light and bouncy.

21 NOTHING BUT WORK

NANCY'S JOURNAL

Why did I say the work here COULD BE WORSE? I spoke
too soon! Now my day is nothing but work.

Mrs Bryce has asked loads of people to tea & dinner
& cocktails & I-don't-know-what. All the folk she has met
in Seaborne these last weeks, I suppose. I had to go all
round The Green putting INVITATIONS through everyone's
letterboxes. That's apart from the ones I took to the Post
Office for stamps. (That should be Alfred's job but he's
driving Cook into town with a shopping list as long as her
arm.)

I bumped into Ella Otter who said her father never ever
goes to anything like that. I thought that very RUDE!! She
tried to tell me something else but I had no time to stop.

When I got back Mrs Bryce was in the Morning Room—
that's where she writes letters—with yet more invitations
in front of her. She gave me a drilling about how to behave.
Taking coats & carrying trays round & so on. Cook's going
to train me to serve ~~gests geust~~ guests properly at the
dinner table. How to spoon up the greens all dainty & not
drop slices of beef on their laps or pour gravy over their
nice white shirt-fronts!

So there won't be time for INVESTIGATING ANYTHING—
or reading—or writing this Journal.

Now I MUST DASH!!

Dear Aunty Bee,

I feel a sneak writing to you like this care of the Bus Depot but I know if I wrote just to you at home Grandma (and Dad—but he won't say) will wonder why & want you to read it out to them.

Please could you send me some money? A Postal Order for £1?? I will pay you back as soon as I can. I PROMISE. It's just that I still haven't had any wages and am down to my last farthing. You gave me some stamps when I left home so I could always write but I'm using the last one for this.

I feel ashamed asking for money. I can't recall if Mrs Bryce said my wages were paid weekly or monthly & don't like to say anything. She is so busy it's not surprising if she has forgotten them. Life down here is a Social Whirl. So much for it being a quiet household like she told me at the start. But I dare say it is monthly so I expect to get them soon. Then I will send you a Postal Order! And that stick of rock I promised.

I have lots of other news but will save it for the next letter to everyone.

Love & a big kiss to you. You are the best Aunty a girl could have!

Nancy

P.S. You can see that I haven't 'borrowed' any more swanky paper. I tore this off the pad Cook keeps for her shopping lists. Though the envelope is Mrs Bryce's I'm afraid.

Dear Nancy,

Just the quickest note to say enclosed please find P.O. for £1/0/0. Of course I have not said a thing to your Gran or your Dad. But you MUST repeat MUST be brave and ask that employer of yours for your wages. It is not fair for her to keep a young girl in her first job short of money like that. Especially when you are far from home. I would have something to say to her if I could meet her!

Your fond Aunt Bee

x

22 TWO GOOD THINGS

NANCY'S JOURNAL

Two Good Things happened today. I am <u>so</u> tired but I really want to write them down before I fall asleep. (& I can't be bothered to look up any spellings!!)

1st: Alfred has found me a BIKE! It was in the back of the garage all covered in cobwebs & he wiped it clean & pumped up the tyres. It's dark blue with the name The Valiant painted in gold letters on the frame. He said 'There you are. You can nip into Seabourne in no time at all on this. If you're feeling VALIANT.'

(I had to look that up in the Dictionary afterwards. It means daring or heroic or brave.)

Just as well then that Wally Green who lives next door to us in Bread Street used to be a bakers boy. He had a BIKE as part of the job & let us kids go on it when he came home for his dinner. Great heavy thing it was—with a big tray on the front. But I managed to pedal up & down the street a few times without falling off before he lost that job (probably for being TOO FREE with the bike) and went to work for the Rat-catcher.

I think I shall have to practiss a bit before I go anywhere on it. No one expects you to look lady-like in Bread Street—but Seabourne's a different matter.

2nd Good Thing: Mr Guy Gommershall is IN THE MOVIES! (That is his name—Guy. So Mrs Bryce's nickname for him is GG, not Gee-Gee as I first thoght.)

Mrs Bryce has just held the first of her parties—that's why I'm tired to death—GG menshunned being in the movies to everyone. I wasn't ear-wigging but he went on so much you couldn't help hearing.

Mrs Bryce's party was EVER SO GRAND. I've never known anything like it. Never dreamed of such a thing!

No tea & cake for Mrs Bryce but champagne cocktails and ices. She hired a Waiter from town just to pour the drinks! My job was to hand out teeny tiny sandwiches & savouries & fruit tarts no bigger than pennies. Cook exelled herself—and we got the left-overs afterwards. My favourite was something called merr-ang.

I had to wear the black frock & a gauzy apron starched so stiff it could have stood up without me. I was a bit nervous—about dropping things mostly. But no one was looking at me. Partly cos —as I discovered—no one takes any notice of us servants. Not even the flashy waiter from Seabourne in his satin waistcoat.

There was hardly anyone I ~~recko~~ reckernized there. Maybe like Professor Otter they turn their noses up at invitations! The only ones I knew were The Finches. They live in that white villa with pink roses all over the front. The girls are pale & willowy with big blue eyes. There is a grown-up son too. They kept hanging round GG. I'm sure they want to be in Movies. They certainly have the looks for it. Except that the son—he is called Timothy Finch—could do with a bit more chin! (I would not say he is actually FROG-FACED—he is too handsome for that.) (Just a little bit froggy.)

Everyone was dressed up & I enjoyed seeing all the fancy outfits. But when Mrs Bryce waltzes in you suddenly notice that beside her all the others look dumpy & frumpy with their fussy frills & gathers.

(It made me stand up straighter & want to be a credit to her.)

Mrs Bryce is like a snake in a dress—an elegant snake—with a great long rope of beads & bare arms & just one single bracelet. She went about being very friendly. I could hear her laughing all the time. Like a quick trill on the piano—I suppose that's what they mean by a Musical Laugh.

She hung on GG's arm & took him round introducing him to everyone. I heard him say that the South Coast is a marvellous place for making films because of the perfect light. Also that people here are not at all stuffy or old-fashunned so it is easy to find EXTRAS who want to join in the crowd scenes. It seemed like everyone he spoke to was very pleased to hear they weren't stuffy or old-fashunned. I didn't know what EXTRAS were but neither did the lady GG was talking to. So he explained— 'EXTRAS are people who fill up the crowd scenes. They dress in costume & must do exactly what the Director tells them to.'

Personally I would ADORE to be an Extra in one of GG's films. (As Aunty Bee always says 'Who knows what might happen???') It could be the beginning of a whole new career!!

(I'm sure I could be a Detective afterwards.) (Or at the same time.)

23 MADE MY DAY

NANCY'S JOURNAL

Good thing I tucked this Journal under my pillow before I fell asleep. 'Cos next I knew Cook was shaking me awake & it was bright daylight outside. Just think if she had found it!!

She said 'Lucky for you the Missus is sleeping late or you'd be for the High Jump.'

As if Mrs Bryce doesn't sleep in late every morning.

Turned out GG was staying in the guest room. He rang the bell about 10 o'clock asking for strong coffee & something to cure a headache. He wore grey silk pyjamas with navy-blue spots on them. (Just imagine Dad in something like that!)

Mrs Bryce had used up all the headache powders so Cook went & fetched some medicine from her room. I'm pretty sure Cook would never poison GG—she is so partial to him. (He was still alive when he left here.)

By the time I took the headache stuff up GG had drunk his coffee & looked much more cheerful. So—heart in my mouth—I said if he was looking for Film Extras any time then I had some EXPERIENSE OF THE THEATRE and would be very willing.

GG tipped his head back & roared with laughter. (Which I don't think you would do if you had a proper headache.)

He said 'Nancy if I ever need a maidservant to walk on with a tray I will come straight to you! You have made my day!!'

He had made my day too by saying that. But I didn't tell him so. I just smiled & bobbed my head & left the room, closing the door without a sound just as Mrs Bryce has trained me to do.

24 LOOT

Stealthily, silently, Horsefield slid his hand into the gap in the rocks—and found the pirate's loot! His fingers closed over the sack. He dragged it towards him.

Mr Cheeseman's voice rang out. 'Quentin! Exactly the lad I wanted to see. I say, what have you got there?'

Quentin stared down at the object he had just pulled out of the hedge—a small drawstring bag patterned with yellow rosebuds. 'Erm—it's—it's my shoe-bag,' he said, and gave Mr Cheeseman his Basilisk Stare.

This was a strategy he'd perfected last term at school. If a teacher came across you somewhere you shouldn't be (like trying to skip Games by hanging about in the boot-room) and you couldn't think of a convincing excuse, you didn't say anything at all. You just stared them straight in the eye, as if—like the Basilisk of ancient myth—you had the power to kill them with a single glance. It (almost) always worked.

It worked on Mr Cheeseman. He looked at the bag, blinked once, and said, 'Ah, yes. Splendid. Now, it's practice night down at the cricket pitch. I'm sure you'd like to meet the other fellows, hit a ball around. Wouldn't you?'

Quentin used his Basilisk Stare again but this time

Mr Cheeseman seemed to be immune. He continued happily, 'You must have got some cricket togs in your school trunk. Run up and get changed, there's a good chap. See you by the front door in five minutes.'

Quentin ran. The rosebud shoe-bag jingled excitingly. He clutched it to his chest to silence it.

He did indeed have cricket togs somewhere in his school trunk. He flung things out haphazardly until he came to them. One thing he flung out was his actual shoe-bag—a completely unembarrassing object made of scuffed canvas, containing his cricket boots. He changed as fast as he could and glanced at the mantelpiece clock. Just time to loosen the neck of the rosebud bag and take a look inside. Through the small opening he made out shining silver, glittering jewels! With a pounding heart and shaking hands he pulled the strings tight again and hid the loot at the very bottom of the trunk.

Mr Cheeseman was waiting for him in the hall, changed and ready for cricket practice.

'We're not exactly the Seabourne First Eleven,' the vicar said, leading the way down the side of the church and into a long shady pathway. 'Sadly the War has depleted our numbers. But we can still get a team up and acquit ourselves decently enough. We're called The All Saints Occasionals. Ha!'

They came out into the evening brightness of a wide green field. At the far end a few figures were gathered. As they got nearer Quentin could see they were either middle-aged men or boys—though the boys were all much bigger than him. The young ones tossed a ball about. The older men stood chatting.

Mr Cheeseman hailed them in a hearty voice. 'Hello,

hello! Brought young Ives along with me, just for fun.'

Quentin winced.

'Where's Alfred tonight?' the vicar asked, as the team gathered round.

'He's busy driving the hire car, Mr Cheeseman,' said a wiry man with a sunburned face. 'Though I'm sure he'd rather be out here with us.'

'Hmm, pity. He's our secret weapon—our demon slow left-hander.'

Quentin smirked as if he knew what this was. He could never remember the rules of cricket or what all the different terms meant.

Mr Cheeseman introduced him round. The last to shake Quentin's hand was a pie-faced young man with small eyes set close together. 'And this is Jim Towner. Or Police Constable Towner, I should say. He's charged with finding our burglar, aren't you, Jim? And all those stolen goods.'

Jim nodded solemnly.

Quentin's stomach did a flip. *Horsefield had been given right into the enemy's hands!*

'What are we waiting for?' cried Mr Cheeseman. 'Let battle commence!'

25 MONEY MATTERS

NANCY'S JOURNAL

Today has been all about MONEY MATTERS. I screwed up my courage like Aunty Bee said & spoke to Mrs Bryce. We worked so hard over the party & Mrs Bryce was pleased with how it went—so I felt it would be the Ideal Time.

I decided to catch her writing letters at her desk so she was sitting down & couldn't just flit away. (She was in a white dress & the sun shone off her smooth bobbed hair & it made me think again how I could easily be working for some FIERCE OLD DRAGON always done up in faded black & reeking of Mothballs or Cough Sweets.)

When I spoke of wages I felt the sweat on the palms of my hands. I wish I could have done good a bit of Acting right then but I was just plain old Nancy Parker aged 14 & 3 $\frac{1}{2}$ weeks, blushing & shaking in my shoes. But Mrs Bryce was very sweet. She gave me the biggest smile, saying 'Oh Nancy what a forgetful creature I am! I'm a little short of cash today but can give you 1 weeks wages for now.' Which she did.

We still did not settle whether I get them once a week or once a month. Mrs Bryce went straight back to her letter writing. At least I've got some coins in my pocket now.

Having to ask for that money put me all in a fluster:

First I broke 2 plates. Only kitchen ones, thank heavens! They just slipped out of my hand while I was drying them. Cook shouted 'Watch your step, my girl!' She said the cost would be STOPPED OUT OF MY WAGES & did not know why that made me laugh.

(She ackused me of cracking a cup once but I swear it was already cracked.)

(I did chip the gravy jug last week but only under the handle where nobody's likely to see it.)

Next I dropped the dustpan & brush all the way down the stairs. It made an awful noise. (Luckily Mrs Bryce had gone out to lunch by then so knew none of this.)

After that I was in such a state that I knocked a wooden box off the writing-desk in the Morning Room. The box is very striking—the lid is painted all over with flowers. I thought Mrs Bryce kept her letters in it but turns out it was full of BILLS. All UNPAID! Butcher, grocer, dressmaker & so forth.

The only ones marked PAID were two bills from Lubbock's Motor Services for the first 2 weeks we were here. I see that she pays through the nose for Alfred & his car. She must think a smart motor is v. important.

SO IT'S NOT ONLY ME THAT MRS BRYCE KEEPS SHORT OF MONEY!

26 THE VALIANT

NANCY'S JOURNAL

I've been out on The Valiant for a proper ride!!! Plus some DETECTING.

Tonight Mrs Bryce was out for dinner & Cook vanished with the evening paper (BEACH DONKEYS STAMPEDE—DAY-TRIPPERS INJURED.) So I changed out of my uniform, got the bike from the garage & slipped away.

I had an IDEA of where I wanted to go. That is if I managed not to fall off 20 times and get myself covered in Blood.

Earlier Alfred said to me 'G̶e̶s̶s̶ Guess where our famous film-maker Mr Guy Gommershall lives?' (I've noticed that Alfred does not care much for GG. Thinks he's a show-off.) I guessed a white mansion on the cliff-top. But Alfred said 'No—in an OLD TAR-PAPER SHACK!'

He found out when he dropped GG home the day after the party. GG said he wanted to walk to clear his muzzy head and got Alfred to drop him at the end of a lane. But the only place that lane leads to—so says Alfred who's lived here all his life—is a couple of rough shacks in the middle of nowhere.

And according to Alfred, his Mum—who's lived here even longer—says nobody ever stays there except NO-GOOD types. The sort that want to keep their business out of sight of prying eyes.

I don't beleeve this for a minute. GG—in his silk pyjamas—living in a wooden shack!

But I had a BURNING DESIRE to investigate and PROVE ALFRED WRONG.

He did say some folk have good reasons for living there. There's a poor fellow called Atwood who was badly wounded in the War & lives at the Shacks cos he doesn't like people staring at him.

So I told Alfred about all the men in London with an arm missing—or a leg missing—or blind. They sell matches outside stations or beg with cardboard signs saying things like GASSED AT YPRES. It always makes me very sad to see them.

It was much further away than I expected. (Aunty Bee always says Country Miles are much longer than Town Miles.) I was quite puffed out.

Then I saw them—just two shacks with nothing but fields all round. They looked as if they had been bilt out of any old left-over thing. One was painted black—walls, roof, even the chimney-pot—but the paint was all Blistered and Peeling. The other one was a patchwork—blue & green & brown & rust—just the colours of the old doors & planks & bits of corrugated iron it was made of.

Round the back was a washing line with shirts and a pair of stripy pyjamas blowing on it. (Not spotted silk ones!) I pictured Mr Gommershall in his showy clothes. I couldn't see him doing his own washing & pegging it out to dry. There was certainly no room in the shack for a Maid. Or a Cook to cook his meals. But Alfred did say Artistic Types don't care a fig for money or what people think so that may account for it. (Seems he knows of a famous painter who lives in a gypsy caravan!!)

No sign of life in the black shack—but a wisp of smoke was coming out of the chimney of the other one. As I got nearer I saw a chair in the porch. Just an ordinary kitchen chair with someone sitting on it.

I wondered if it was GG but he was in the shadow of the porch & I couldn't see clearly. Anyway—whoever it was—as I drew close they got up and went inside. I would say they HURRIED INSIDE. Sort of furtive. (Maybe Alfred's Mum is right.)

I must say I did get _wobbly_ then. Tho it may have been that the ground there was very stony & hard to ride over.

Soon after the track came to an end, with just a gate & a load of sheep on the far side. I could smell the sea & the wind was blustering about like fury. There was a winding path thru some thistles but it was just where somebody—or the sheep—had walked. It didn't look like it would lead to a sparkling white MANSION. Or anywhere really.

It felt silly turning the bike round straight away if the Mystery Man had seen me go past—which he must have.

That's why he shot indoors. So I stood there for a bit pretending to admire the view as if that's why I was there. But I had to ride back. There wasn't any other way to go. From that side the Shacks didn't look too bad. (An Artistic Type like GG might well think it a PICTURE-ESK sort of place to stay.)

As I went past I saw the man again, looking out. Definitly not GG. His face was all dark and wrinkled as if his skin had been roasted. So he must be the man Alfred talked about who was ~~dissfig~~ disfigerred in the War.

I rode as fast as I could without falling off—I knew I'd been out far too long. When I got back Cook was in a right old mood. 'WHERE ON EARTH HAVE YOU BEEN, GIRL?!'

I said I'd nipped out for some fresh air but didn't tell her I went on a bike. I don't think she saw me put it away because the garage is at the side of the house & the kitchen windows face the back.

So I have been VALIANT. Being able to ride a bike makes you feel like that!

Next thing I will be driving a motor car—or flying an air-o-plane!!

(But I still don't know for sure about GG.)

27 MURDER, THAT'S WHAT!

Ella sat on her favourite tombstone, kicking her heels and waiting. She had laid another sign for Nancy, out in the lane. This one was made of pine cones and some great big daisies that grew by the churchyard wall. It was in the shape of a

and she thought it rather beautiful.

She peered up into the cedar tree. No sign of spies this afternoon. The church clock chimed quarter to five. As the sound died away a face appeared around the lychgate: Nancy's. And another, lower down: Sausage.

Nancy called out, 'Don't worry. I kicked your sign out the way so no one else will spot it.'

Ella felt a slight pang. It had been a very good sign.

Nancy sat next to her while Sausage snuffled his way happily through the grass. 'What did you want to see me for?'

Ella leaned close and lowered her voice. 'I know who

the robber is! Miss Dearing told me. You were right. Do you remember what you said?'

Nancy shook her head.

'About the thief having a magpie eye?'

Nancy nodded.

'He is a magpie—a real one that Miss Dearing rescued.'

Nancy folded her arms and looked rather pleased.

Ella went on, 'He did what magpies do and took a fancy to shiny things. Whenever he saw one within easy reach, he grabbed it and flew off with it. Took it home. Miss Dearing's got him in a cage now, so that he can't steal anything else. But it's all a deadly secret—you mustn't breathe a word. You see, Miss Dearing doesn't dare own up. She's afraid if people find out about his bad habits they'll take Marius away from her. Most probably wring his neck! She only told me because she wants me to give all the stolen goods back to their owners.'

'You?'

'Yes. Because I know exactly what belongs to whom. She saw me with my notebook after I'd spoken to Miss La Roche. She wanted me to put the things back secretly. Without the owners noticing how they got there.' Ella rolled her eyes to show the extreme difficulty of this.

Nancy said, 'So—did you?'

'No! Because here's the frightful thing . . .'

Ella paused for effect. Nancy's eyes widened. Even Sausage stopped sniffing the ground below their feet and looked up.

'It's gone. The entire store of stolen goods—vanished! Miss Dearing entrusted them to me in a bag and I didn't know what to do at first, so I hid it. Now it's gone.

Someone's taken it.'

'Oh, heck! Who? And what are you going to do?'

'Not sure. I can't face telling her I've lost the stuff. Not until I've tried my utmost to find it. What do you think we should do next?'

'We? You're not dragging me into this. I've got my own—'

Ella interrupted her. 'But you understand. You like detective stories. You know what I'm talking about!'

And there's no one else, Ella thought. She couldn't tell her father or Mrs Prebble—they would just dismiss it as silly nonsense, or make her confess everything to Dozy Jim. Nancy had become an almost—sort of—friend.

'Listen,' Nancy said, jumping off the tomb and picking up Sausage's lead from the grass, 'it's not as if that missing stuff is ancient treasure or priceless ruby necklaces. From what I see, people around here can easily afford to replace those bits and pieces if you can't get them back. It's not a serious crime. Not like what's going on at—'

'What else is going on? Where?'

But Nancy said no more, just seized the dog and tucked him under her arm. She strode away, making for the gate. Ella ran after her.

'What do you mean?'

Nancy whirled round. They were face to face now in the shadows of the lychgate.

'Murder, that's what!' she hissed. 'A murderer—right under my own roof.'

If she said any more it was drowned by the church clock chiming five. When it stopped Nancy was gone and Ella just stood there, open-mouthed.

28 THE ROSEBUD BAG

Quentin shut his bedroom door—which had a lock, but no key—and jammed a chair under the handle. He tested it. No one could get in. Then he pulled the clinking rosebud bag out of his school trunk and shook its contents over the bedspread.

So disappointing! Only the most ordinary assortment—no gold or jewels. He winkled out a glittery brooch from the heap. The biggest stone was chipped: not diamond, only glass. He tested a paper-knife on his fingertip—so blunt it made barely a dent. There was a silver teaspoon just like the ones the Cheesemans used. What was it That Girl had said about missing teaspoons and burying rock buns? He slipped the spoon into his pocket. He could put it back in the dining-room drawer when he went downstairs and nobody would be any the wiser. But what on earth could he do with the rest of the stuff? He couldn't simply hide the bag in the hedge again, not when Mr Cheeseman had already seen him clutching the wretched thing.

If it were gold and jewels, antique pistols and gem-studded daggers, he'd be happy to say he'd recovered the entire haul and take the credit. But this lot looked more like jumble.

As to solving the crimes, it was That Girl who'd hidden the bag in the vicarage hedge. He was more or less sure: he'd seen an Ella-like shape and size scrabbling about on the other side of the thick bushes. He hadn't been able to resist finding out what she was up to; when he spotted the bag the puzzle just got more mysterious. And she had that map of the crime scenes in her notebook, complete with numbers and arrows! But he didn't think she was the actual thief. Would a thief keep notes which could incriminate them?

Quentin could have said something to Jim Towner when he met him at the cricket field. Looking back, that would have been the easiest solution. Constable Towner could have accompanied him to the vicarage right away and Quentin could have handed over the bag. Except that he would have blushed beetroot-red when explaining— enough to make him look guilty. And had he told the vicar or Mrs Cheeseman what he had found? No, he had hidden it deep in his school trunk—that looked guilty too. He had even lied to Mr Cheeseman about the bag! None of this looked like the acts of an innocent person.

John Horsefield would have managed this far better.

But of course Quentin couldn't be blamed for the crimes! He had only recently come to Seabourne, and the robberies had been going on for . . . Quentin realized he had no idea when they started. Supposing it was only after he arrived? What if residents of The Green began to notice items going missing just about the time that strange boy arrived at the vicarage? A strange boy who later turned out to have the bag of loot tucked away in his bedroom?!

With shaking hands he scooped the stolen goods

together and shoved them back into the bag. However he framed his version of events, it still stank like a bucket of rotting fish. The safest thing he could do would be to get rid of the bag and all it held—but where?

29 WAGGING TONGUES

NANCY'S JOURNAL

Ella Otter was round first thing this morning. Yesterday I left her on—what they call in a book—a cliff-hanger. We snuck into the garage to talk cos Cook was busy having a blazing row with the Butcher's boy over a bill & Alfred wasn't here.

I told Ella my Theory about Cook. She didn't laugh or look like she didn't believe me. She looked ALERT. Like Sausage when he hears an interesting noise. (Interesting to dogs <u>that is</u>. Often I can't hear a thing.)

She had a think & this is what she came up with. I have to say is HER MIND IS QUICK.

Ella's ideas:—

Cooks often call themselves 'Mrs' even tho they aren't married. It's called a CURTESY TITLE because they have an important job in a household. Mrs Prebble who is their Housekeeper is not really a MRS. But she has been with them for years—since long before Ella was born & her mother died—and they call her that out of respect. So Cook may <u>never</u> have had a husband.

I didn't know about Ella's mother dying. She said it happened when she was a baby & too young to remember so it wasn't sad for her. She is buried in America but Prof. Otter put up a beutiful window in the church here in memory of her. Ella said I could go in ANY TIME to look.

So then I told her about my Mum and how I was six when she got sick and I could remember her a bit.

(I didn't say I wish my Mum had a church window to remember her by.)

(I will go and take a look.)

Ella's ideas (continued):—

Why Cook may have hated Mrs Bryce's husbands. They may have been:-

cruel

or drunkards

or spent all the money

or ALL THREE.

I didn't think Mr Bryce at least had spent all his money cos Mrs Bryce still has lots. Ella said 'It could be HER OWN money. Mr Bryce could have married her for it and run thru lots of it before he died.'

(Which goes to show I know nothing about money.) (Never having had any.)

She asked if the Dark Secret was that Cook had killed the husbands off! (That was before I even got to the end of my Theory.) She clutched my hand then in the darkness of the garage & we nearly screamed.

Because we both thoght the SAME THING!

Next we were both struck by the same thing again: if Cook saw that Mr Bryce was spending all his wife's money—leaving poor Mrs B. penniless & up to her eyes in dett—that was a very good reason to bump him off before he spent any more.

123

'THE MOTIVE!' Ella shouted—so loud I had to stick my hand over her mouth.

She said I must get into Cook's room again & find out what's in those bottles. If I give her a list she will look up the names & check for Poisons.

The book about medicines and illnesses might help Cook work out how to poison people while making it look like a genuine illness.

Maybe Cook is Thin With Worry. Worry she will be FOUND OUT. (This sounds very convincing to me.)

Then Ella asked me:—

Did I know why Mrs Bryce came to the coast? & why choose Seabourne in particular?

I told her both Mrs Bryce & Cook <u>hate</u> GOSSIP—& they never tell me their business either. (I only know that GG thinks Seabourne is a perfect place to make a film becos I overheard him.) But it seems people have been gossiping about Mrs Bryce.

Ella said that Mrs Prebble said that Mrs Bryce may be here to Hunt for a Husband. People used to do that before the War & they are doing it again. Specially now men are in such SHORT SUPPLY. Seaside Resorts are the perfect place to meet a future husband or wife cos everyone is jolly & looking their best & out to have a good time. There are loads of places to meet at tea & dancing & tennis & golf & so on.

I said 'And parties.' It all made perfect sense.

Ella then wanted to know:—

If she gets a new husband will Cook bump him off?
Is that part of the plan?

'Poor Mrs Bryce' I said. I meant it. But then Ella said

'Or are they IN IT TOGETHER??? To find a rich man to marry and then do away with him?' (That's when we clutched hands again.)

I find that hard to beleve of Mrs B. but we had no time to discuss it further for the Butcher's Boy came stamping past in a vile mood & I had to dash.

I came up to my room & wrote all this down as soon as I could.

Oh but I did say to Ella as she darted off that she should investigate that boy with the glasses who was always sneaking round. That's if she wanted to find out what became of the BAG OF STOLEN GOODS. She made such a face when I told her that.

Names on Poison Bottles

Gentian Violet

Phosferine

Camphor

Tincture of Mullein

Oil of Cloves

Witchhazel

Glauber's Salts

Syrup of Figs

Dr Aleyn's Corn Paint

30 NOT P****** AT ALL

NANCY'S JOURNAL

I crept back into Cook's room to get the names on the Poison bottles. Also I had another look at that case under the bed—and this time it WAS LOCKED!

Does this mean Cook is suspicious of me?? Did I leave some clue last time that I had been in there? I am going to have to BE VERY CAREFUL.

(I wish I could write this Detective Diary in Secret Code—but I don't know any & if I made one up it would take a very long time to write things down & to read them back.) (And I might forget it.)

Not long after I slipped that list to Ella I found an envelope addressed to me shoved thru the letterbox. I will tuck it in here. Given that she has never been to School her handwriting is very neat!

Dear Nancy,

Just to let you know I have looked up all the P****** you listed in both a Medical Dictionary and 'The Comprehensive Herbal of Plants Ancient & Modern & Their Uses' and found they are not P****** at all.

I asked Mrs Prebble, too. I did not have to explain to her why I wanted to know. She is used to me.

Each one is a remedy for everyday ailments such as toothache, coughs, burns or blisters. For instance, Glauber's Salts and Syrup of Figs are to aid a sluggish digestion. (Mrs Prebble recommends the last one.)

Mrs Prebble also says that they would be a useful set of remedies to keep in the home. The only one she has not come across is Dr Aleyn's Corn Paint, but she is thinking of looking into that as she suffers from painful corns herself. On her little toes.

Yours sincerely,

E. Otter

P.S. I decided it was the wisest course not to write the word out in full just in case this letter is intercepted.
P.P.S. I can see that this is a disappointing result.

She is right about the last thing.

May have to think again regarding my Theory About Cook. If she doesn't use Poison what other murder method does she use? Is that why she reads so much about DEATH in the papers? To get ideas???

31 JUMBLE

Mr Cheeseman was off to the hospital to visit a sick parishioner.

'Quentin,' he said, 'I've left you a set of Latin exercises and the title of a four-page essay I'd like you to write on Oliver Cromwell.'

Mrs Cheeseman was off to Mrs Finch's house for a meeting of the Ladies' Flower Committee, which was in charge of decorating the church.

'Quentin,' she said. 'I've brought you a glass of milk and two ginger biscuits.' Then she pulled on a hat exactly like a squashed mushroom and went out.

Quentin downed the milk in one go. He stuffed the biscuits into the pocket of his school shorts, and hid behind the study curtain as Mrs Cheeseman crunched away over the gravel and headed for The Green. Then he too left the house.

Stealthily, silently, Horsefield took his chance.

Inside the vestry he soon found the huge box where Mrs Cheeseman kept the jumble sale offerings, and began pulling things out. They were tangled up and rather disgusting. He flung them to the floor and went on digging. But what was this? A boy's shirt of thin blue cotton with short sleeves. He tried it on—over his own school shirt, of course. He wasn't going to undress in the vestry. Someone might come in! The shirt was only slightly too big, but then that would make it billowing and cool. Next he unearthed a pair of wrinkled summer shorts. The elastic belt had a silver metal fastening just like a snake's head! He'd always wanted one of those. He pulled the shorts on. They were only slightly too tight—but then he did have his sturdy school shorts on beneath them. He was sure they would do.

He was just about to shuffle out of them again when a noise stopped him. A noise from within the church. He waited, and listened.

The noise came again, most definitely in the nave. Footsteps. And—something else. Whistling! Cheerful whistling. In church. What if it was that burglar back again, come to pinch the church silver this time?!

He pushed the vestry door open a crack and peered out. The door creaked. Quentin froze.

The man spun round and was lit by a beam of sun falling through the south windows. His dark hair was slicked back and his finely-chiselled features, Quentin noted, were those of a hero. Not far from what he imagined John Horsefield to look like.

'Hallo there!' the man called out. 'I wonder if you can help me?'

'Me?' Quentin edged halfway out of the vestry door.

'Just admiring the church. P'raps you can tell me a bit about it?' He had a casual, drawling voice, and he put his hands in his pockets as if he was perfectly at home.

Quentin edged fully out.

'Very handsome place,' the stranger went on. 'Lots of plaques and memorials to the good old families living hereabouts. Islings. Wellbeloveds. Either of those your name?' He flashed a film-star smile.

'No. I'm Quentin Ives. I'm from the vicarage.'

'Oh, so you will know a thing or two! This one, fr'instance.' The visitor waved his arm at the Isling memorial, a large brass plaque in a prominent place on the wall.

'There's a great big tomb of theirs out in the churchyard,' Quentin said. 'The Islings owned much of the farmland round here. Sold for housing now, and for the airfield.' He was surprised at how much he remembered of the local history Mr Cheeseman had taught him. Probably because the vicar had promised him a visit to the airfield. They hadn't been there yet. 'It was built during the War, but it's still there, as a civil airport. Pleasure trips over the bay, mainly. But planes fly up to Croydon and across to France.'

'The Islings must be very rich,' the stranger said.

'I think they're very dead, these days,' said Quentin.

'What about the Wellbeloveds?'

'The last Wellbeloved was killed in the War.' Quentin was beginning to feel a bit of an expert. He stepped out into the church's main aisle and pointed with a sweep of his arm to a sad, simple marble tile on the wall. 'That's all about him. Only twenty-three. His poor widowed mother's gone away. Can't bear the memories left here.'

He had made that last bit up, but he was enjoying himself. At Easter his mother had taken him to see a play at the town hall. It was only the local Amateur Dramatics Society but the performance was rather stirring and for a day or two Quentin toyed with the idea of becoming an actor. Right now he felt he had all the necessary qualities.

'Anything else of note?' prompted the stranger. 'Any grand personage I've missed?'

'There's this,' Quentin told him. His favourite window—made of blue and sea-green and daffodil-yellow stained glass, and designed by a famous artist whose name he couldn't actually remember—was dedicated to someone called Lavinia Otter. She died young, Mr Cheeseman had said: a tragic story. Quentin escorted the stranger over to it. The sun was shining through and the window looked its very best. He rested his hands on his new trouser belt and said in an authoritative way, 'Er, Snakeshead designed that, you know. Very famous artist. Very typical of his style.'

'You don't say?' The man leaned back to admire it. 'Snakeshead, eh?' He nodded, as if he knew the name.

'The Otters live just over The Green. Professor Otter—he's an archaeologist. Always digging up Roman treasure and hoards of Saxon gold, that sort of stuff.'

'Is he, now? Well, well.'

'Can't move in their house for priceless artefacts. He's famous all over the world. When he's not digging stuff up he writes books about it,' Quentin added, just to make sure the man was impressed. He remembered something else Mrs Cheeseman had said. 'In America the Otters made their millions in the railways, but the Professor came to England because he doesn't like anything too modern-day. We've got lots of old ruins for him here.'

The man whistled a long low note. 'Millions, eh?'

Above them in the tower the church clock began to strike midday.

'Time to go,' said the man. 'Thanks awfully, old chap. You've been a mine of information.'

Feeling a glow of proprietorship, Quentin walked with him to the church door. He flung it wide and the sun poured in.

The man turned one last time. Quentin waited for his next compliment.

'Aren't you rather hot in that get-up, though?'

Quentin looked down at himself and remembered to his horror that he was wearing a jumble sale shirt a bit too big and jumble sale shorts a bit too small. The long sleeves and long legs of his school uniform poked out from underneath.

The stranger strolled away, whistling again.

32 ENEMY FLAG

'That boy who's always sneaking round,'—of course he was the one to spot her stuffing contraband into the vicarage hedge. That's where Ella had first observed him, peering round the end of it. Nancy's advice made complete sense.

But today The Boy was nowhere to be seen. He wasn't lurking in the churchyard or skulking round The Green and Ella couldn't hear any noise of bats hitting balls in the vicarage garden. She made sure that Miss Dearing was nowhere in sight, either, then crunched up the gravel drive with an air of great determination.

Mrs Cheeseman answered the door. She was red in the face. Smudges of flour decorated her nose and chin.

'Oh, have I interrupted you in the middle of something?' Ella asked.

Mrs Cheeseman swiped at her floury nose and said, crossly, 'Yes, as a matter of fact you have. I'm making pastry. What did you want?'

'It's utterly imperative that I speak to Quentin Ives.'

'Quentin is having lessons with the vicar. They cannot possibly be disturbed.'

'When do lessons finish?'

'Not until four o'clock. Then there's cricket practice.

Then there's tea.'

'I'll come back after tea, then.'

Mrs Cheeseman still looked put out, although Ella felt she had been perfectly reasonable.

'If you wish. Goodbye.'

Ella found herself looking at the flaking paint on the vicarage door.

Quentin lurked behind the study curtain, watching That Girl trudge away out of sight. He was pretty sure he knew what she had come for. Him. She must know he had the rosebud bag. For the first time he was glad of Mrs Cheeseman's strict manner with callers. But he had to act—and fast.

Across the desk, Mr Cheeseman was trying to write his weekly column for the Parish Newsletter. He crossed out three or four headings and scribbled the opening paragraph twice, then struck a line through it. Sighing, he threw down his pen and said, 'The air's like soup in here. It's too hot to think. What say we go outside and chuck a cricket ball about? Nip up to your room and fetch your cricket pads. I'll get changed and meet you outside in ten minutes.'

The thought of cricket practice in the garden didn't fill Quentin with quite so much dread these days. Recently he'd hit more balls than he missed. Mr Cheeseman had begun to say, 'Nice try,' 'Well played,' and even—once— 'Good shot!', despite the fact that the ball was winging its way towards his greenhouse.

Quentin grinned—but not about cricket. He'd just

had a thought. Ten minutes. That was enough to do it. Two minutes across to the church, two minutes inside, two minutes to get back.

He dashed up to his room, rootled in the trunk and came up with the yellow rosebud bag. He hated the way it clinked and rattled now. He enclosed it between his stiff cricket knee-pads, tucked them under his arm, and leapt down the back stairs two at a time. *Cunningly concealing the treasure, John Horsefield made his escape.* He could hear Mrs Cheeseman slamming plates and banging pans in the kitchen. The back door opened noiselessly. No one was about. He ran, low and quick, across the garden and into the churchyard.

The iron ring of the side door turned under his hand. The vestry was a sudden pool of darkness after the sunshine. But he knew what he was looking for—the box of jumble. Pawing heaps of wool and cotton aside, he tumbled the contents of the rosebud bag out into the middle, gave everything a mighty stir, and then stuffed the bag itself right down into the bottom.

Mission accomplished.

When Ella returned she ran into Mrs Cheeseman coming out of the gate. Mrs Cheeseman stepped lightly and looked in a better mood, face scrubbed clean, and wearing her familiar squashed-mushroom hat.

'Quentin is in the garden,' she warbled. 'You can find your own way, can't you, Ella? I'm dashing off to a meeting of the Jumble Sale Committee.'

Ella discovered Quentin lounging on a rug on the

lawn. He was reading a comic and dipping into a bowl of cherries. She watched him put one in his mouth, spit the stone into his palm and toss it into the flowerbed without a glance.

'Quentin Ives!'

Ella enjoyed seeing him jump. She stalked across the lawn and stood, silent, glaring down at him. Quentin pretended by the careless way he kept on with the comic and the cherries that he had no idea why she was there.

'I know you've got it.'

Quentin gave her a strange look. Ella took no notice. 'What have you done with it?' she demanded.

Quentin took a handful of cherries and put them in his mouth so that he couldn't speak. He went on staring.

'I hope you swallow them, stones and all, and a cherry tree sprouts in your insides!'

Quentin gagged and coughed a mess of dark red goo and light brown stones into his cupped hand. 'That's impossible. Scientifically speaking,' he said thickly. He lobbed the lot into the roses and wiped his hand on a handkerchief. It still looked gore-stained when he'd finished.

He leant back on one elbow in a casual way. 'I do know what you mean, as it happens. The bag full of stolen things. You had it and I saw you hide it in the hedge.'

Ella narrowed her eyes and said nothing.

Quentin went on, 'And you're the one who drew a map of the village. With certain houses marked.'

Was he trying to use Psychology on her? How dare he!

'If you really saw that map, you'd know what it was for. But I don't suppose you could make head or tail of it!'

'I could, as a matter of fact.' He turned over the next page of the comic as if he was still reading. Ella knew he wasn't.

She abandoned Psychology herself and stamped her foot. 'Why are you so horrid? Give the bag back! I need it.'

'I haven't got it.'

'I know you have.'

'I haven't got it *any more*.'

Ella snatched the comic out from under his nose. She wanted to rip it into dramatic tiny pieces but it looked quite interesting. Father never let her buy comics. So she held it behind her back.

'Where is it?'

Quentin shrugged and sighed. 'Gone. Just gone. Oh, except for Mrs Cheeseman's teaspoon, which I put back in the drawer.'

'Gone where?'

'Where no one will be able to trace it back to me. Or you.'

'Where? Is? It?'

'Not telling. But no one will find it for ages.'

'I have to know.'

'Best that you don't. Safest that way.' Quentin sat up straight as if he meant business, and held out his hand for the comic. 'You see, if you don't know, no one can torture the information out of you.'

It did make perfect sense. Ella had to admit that. But it was so—grrr!—frustrating. Giving Quentin her most evil glare, she turned and ran away across the vicarage lawn, around the house, and up the driveway. She bore the comic home like a stolen enemy flag.

33 LITTLE BLACK BOOK

NANCY'S JOURNAL

Mrs Bryce dropped her notebook in the hall today on her way out—the little black one with the silver pencil. When she isn't writing in it she keeps it in her handbag. I didn't spot it until after she'd gone. So I decided to look inside. It is really MY DUTY to know.

It was a Great Diserpointment however. I was hoping to find out some big secrets (like she would find if she read my Diary!!) But there was not a word about Mr Treadgold or Mr Bryce. (I suppose that is all a long time ago now.) Nothing about Cook either. Tho Mrs Bryce has little tiny writing which can be very hard to read.

The pages I could make out were just LISTS OF THINGS, some crossed out or with ticks & stars beside them. I reckernized some of the names from those invitations I had to post. So it must be all about the parties Mrs Bryce gives & the ones she goes to. Who she meets & who she wants to meet. (We've got another big day coming up—a tea-party & all the neybours are invited. So I haven't got much time to write this down.)

THE NEWEST LIST WENT:—

☆ Prof. Otter
☆ Maj. Corcoran
☆☆☆ Mr Avery-Atkins
☆ T. Finch

and they all had stars beside them.

What struck me right away was—is this a list of possible HUSBANDS?

Why it might be:—

Major Corcoran lives in the house like a castle & I have never seen a woman coming out or going in. He has a man-servant to look after him, a stuck-up looking fellow who never says Good Day. He is therefore RICH and UNMARRIED. But he is <u>very old</u>.

Professor Otter had a wife (Ella's mum) but she died years ago. (I don't know if he is rich.) (Not if his appearance is anything to go by.)

No idea who Mr Avery-Atkins is. But I can make a good guess: RICH & FREE TO MARRY. He had ☆☆☆!

T. Finch must be Mrs Finch's son Timothy. He is a bit young—I would say about 18 or 19—tho he is by far the best-looking (despite having no chin). The Finches have lots of snooty maids in smart uniforms and a big black motor car. Therefore = RICH.

(I wonder why she doesn't want to marry Mr Gommershall? He is even handsomer & more like the right age.)

There was another page which said something like:—

~~South Coast Film Company~~

~~Coastal Picture Co.~~

~~Blue Skies Film Co.~~

Blue Sky Motion Pictures

~~Wide Skies Motion Pictures~~

No idea what this was for (except it's about Film

Companies.) Maybe the ones Mrs Bryce crossed out are no good.

Tucked in with it there was a loose page in different handwriting & signed just G. I only saw it when it fell out. I have kept it. I'm sure Mrs B will never notice it's gone. For someone SO FUSSY she is quite CARELESS.

I put the notebook on the desk in the Morning Room where Mrs Bryce often writes. I hope she will think she just left it there & forgot. I didn't want her to suspeckt I had been snooping.

I am quite pleased that I could remember those lists. I think I have recalled them correctly.

A GOOD MEMORY is vital to being a good Detective.

(Nancy Parker's Theory of Detection No. 3)

It's just struck me that Mrs Bryce is VERY MIXED UP with this film business. I do wonder if she will make it difficult when the filming is underway if GG asks me to be an Extra. I bet she won't want to spare me from housework and door-opening duties. She must let me. It is my first BIG CHANCE!

Almost there now.
Blue Skies here we come!

G x

34 PROFESSOR OTTER ACCEPTS AN INVITATION

Ella had never seen such a dauntingly huge crowd at a tea party before. Her father hesitated in the doorway. 'I'm only here because you twisted my arm,' he murmured. 'We'll stay awhile to be polite, then make our escape!'

Before he could take a step, Mrs Bryce swooped down on them with a dazzling smile. 'Professor Otter! I'm delighted that you decided to tear yourself away from your work and join us!'

The professor looked startled. He cleared his throat and said, 'Good afternoon, Mrs Bryce. May I present my daughter?'

Ella stuck out her hand. 'Eleanor Mary Otter.'

Her name had not been on the invitation but she didn't care. This was the perfect chance for some serious Anthropology, and she might even find out something to help with Nancy's theory about the cook.

Mrs Bryce ignored Ella's hand. Her laugh trilled upwards but Ella could tell she wasn't amused. 'I'm afraid it's a grown-up party, Eleanor. There aren't any other little children here to keep you company. Perhaps you'd like to run around in the garden?' Then she seized Professor Otter by the arm and swept him away. 'There's someone here you must meet . . .'

Ella stared after them. She didn't trust that tinkling laugh or that dazzling smile. Not one bit. Nancy had strong suspicions about the cook, but Ella began to wonder about Mrs Bryce.

'Would you like tea or lemonade, miss?'

Ella jumped. Nancy had slid silently right up beside her. Her face was quite blank.

'Tea or lemonade to drink, miss?'

'Oh, lemonade, please. Why are you calling me miss?'

Nancy dropped her voice. 'It's what I've been trained to do. You're a guest and I'm just the maid.'

'Unwanted guest,' Ella muttered. 'Your Mrs Bryce made that very clear!'

Mrs Cheeseman approached and Nancy slipped away.

'Ella—hello! If I'd known children were to be here I'd have brought Quentin. I can recommend the shrimp pastries, by the way—scrumptious.'

Ella smiled and said nothing. The last thing she needed was The Boy hanging about and getting in her way. She wanted a good look around the inside of Cliffe Lodge. Her gaze followed Mrs Bryce, fluttering in her pale yellow gown like a brimstone butterfly amongst the dowdier guests. Wherever she went the laughter rose.

Nancy came back with a glass of lemonade on a silver tray. 'Would you like a sandwich or a savoury, miss? Or there's strawberry shortcake.'

'Mrs Prebble always makes me eat plain bread-and-butter before I can have any cake.'

'Mrs Prebble isn't here—and nobody's looking.'

It was true. Those who weren't busy piling their plates were glancing about in an expectant way, as if something thrilling was about to happen. Their eyes kept flicking back to Mrs Bryce and the tall handsome man she was introducing around.

'Who's that?' Ella asked.

'Mr Guy Gommershall. He's something big in the movie business.'

'Is that why everyone who's not busy stuffing their faces is trying to catch his eye?'

Nancy spoke out of the side of her mouth. Her face had returned to its glaze of blankness. 'He's looking for somewhere to make his next film, and Mrs Bryce says he should choose Seabourne. I hope he does.'

'It looks like everyone wants him to choose to Seabourne!'

Mrs Cheeseman came back in search of more treats. Nancy quickly took up her station by the tea table again.

Ella filled a plate, watched closely by Mrs Bryce's dog. She edged a miniature cheese straw off her plate. Sausage gulped it down. She flicked him a pastry topped with something a bit like squishy frogspawn. That vanished too.

Over the excited chatter Ella heard Miss La Roche's penetrating voice say, 'It's my belief that everything people thought was stolen has just been mislaid!'

Ella stopped. Miss Dearing—exactly the person she had hoped to avoid—stood at Miss La Roche's elbow, listening avidly. But Ella had to know more.

Miss La Roche swept on. 'I simply did not notice that the thimble was still on my finger. It must have slid off when I put my hand into the pocket of my gardening apron. And there it stayed, hidden away, all this time! All the rumours flying about made me assume it had been stolen.'

'You just lost it?' Miss Dearing said, in a faint voice.

'Yes. I made the evidence fit the crime. Yet there was no crime! Has anyone seen this criminal? No! So, I do believe the rumours of robbery have no basis in fact. People are careless, or forgetful, or both.'

Mrs Cheeseman chipped in. 'Do you know, I counted up my best set of teaspoons again—and there aren't any missing!'

'Voilà,' said Miss La Roche. 'I knew I was right.' She gestured so emphatically that she knocked Mrs Cheeseman's second helping of shrimp pastries to the floor. Sausage was on them in a flash. He left no evidence at all.

Ella felt a sharp grip on her arm. Miss Dearing hissed in her ear, 'Excellent work! You've started to return everything and no one suspects a thing.'

Ella didn't know what to say. Miss La Roche might be right about her own case—she did have a terrible memory, and a very vivid imagination. Ella hadn't spotted any thimble in Marius's hoard. She *had* seen the silver teaspoon. Quentin said he put that back. But as for the rest, Miss Dearing would discover soon enough that nothing else was turning up and then what would happen? Quentin told her he'd hidden it where nobody could trace it back to them. What on earth could he mean?

35 LETTIE & LITTLE MAY

Miss Dearing let her go and Ella slipped away to examine her surroundings. Cliffe Lodge was a rented furnished house, not a personal one. The only things that might give any information about its inhabitants were the photographs displayed on the mantelpiece. Ella stood on tiptoe and peered.

There was Mrs Bryce, lithe and sporty, in a group of tennis players, and one of her in a deckchair with Sausage in her arms: both recent snaps, by the look of it. Another was of a wedding party. Ella took it down and examined it. No one in the crowd resembled Mrs Bryce, even under the big hats and fussy hair fashionable a few years ago. There was also a posed portrait of a stiff old couple—Mrs Bryce's parents?—though again, Ella could find no likeness at all. She reached for a picture of a smart middle-aged man in uniform. It slipped from her fingers with a clink and a crash. Whoever he was, now he lay in smithereens upon the hearth-tiles.

In an instant Nancy was beside her. 'I'll fetch a dustpan.'

'I couldn't help it,' Ella said. 'It just sort of fell apart!'

'Never mind, I don't think anyone noticed over all the noise. And the missus is far too busy, out on the terrace, showing off Mr Gommershall. I'll say a guest accidently broke it but I won't say who.'

While she was gone Ella examined the photograph. On the front—at the bottom where it had been covered by the frame—were scrawled two lines of handwriting. The ink was faded but Ella could just make out:

To dearest Lettie & little May,
With love, Leonard xx June 1908

When Nancy came back with the dustpan-and-brush she asked, 'Who is this supposed to be?'

'I always got the impression it was Mr Bryce.'

'But look at the message.'

Nancy read it and frowned. 'I don't think he looks much like a Leonard, do you? Too handsome and silvery. More like a Harry or a Gerald.'

'That's hardly the point,' Ella said, turning the photograph over. On the back was an oval stamp with the words Milton Sharpe Photographic Studios, Epsom, Surrey in the middle. 'What's Mrs Bryce's first name?'

'Mr Gommershall calls her Connie.'

'You've never heard her referred to as Lettie?'

'Never.'

'And who d'you think Little May is?'

'May be another pet she had before Sausage . . . But it sounds more like a girl's name than a dog's.'

'I agree. Don't you think this is suspicious?'

Nancy stood up, the dustpan full of glass. 'I don't know . . .'

'If it's her late husband why is it scrawled over with love to someone else?'

'I might have got it wrong and he's not Mr Bryce at all. Got to go now—I daren't spend too long away from the tea table. People will notice.'

Ella hissed after her, 'Can you find out if Mr Bryce's name was Leonard? And did they ever live in Epsom? It's vital to the case!'

'Which case?' Nancy hissed back.

'Whatever it is we're investigating here. I'm beginning to think Mrs Bryce has a past she's hiding, too!'

36 SOMETHING BIG IN THE MOVIE BUSINESS

'Ella! There you are!'

Ella's father gave her a pleading look. He needed rescuing. He was tucked in a corner, with Mr Guy Gommershall towering over him.

Mr Gommershall was saying, 'Wonder if you ever thought of capturing an archaeological dig with a moving camera? Certainly make a marvellous film! I've heard all about the hoards of gold that you dig up.'

Professor Otter gave a quiet laugh. 'Gold—hardly! I doubt the general public would be very excited by what we dig up.'

Ella loved his gentle voice, sounding more American than usual amongst the English tea-party chatter. He was very polite but, underneath, very stubborn.

Guy Gommershall went smoothly on. 'Is it true that you prefer Old England to the New World, Professor, even though your family's fortune was made in America?'

'It is. Otters have always loved new-fangled things. They built railroads and now they're building motor cars. Indeed, my cousin Cosway has just invented a new kind of tyre. I guess I'm the exception to the rule.'

Ella slipped in at her father's side. Now was the time to try Psychology. She opened her eyes wide and looked as foolish as she could. 'Have you been in Seabourne long, Mr Gommershall? Are you on holiday here?'

Guy Gommershall guffawed—another fake laugh, Ella thought. 'The answer's no to both those questions. Darling Connie tipped me off about Seabourne. She knew I'd adore it.'

Darling Connie, Ella noted. Not Dearest Lettie.

She kept grinning away as if she was spellbound and Mr Gommershall went on, 'I'm in the movie business, you see, and this place could be just the spot for my next film. Connie's keen for me to set up an office and start organizing the production straight away.'

She blinked innocently at him. 'How did you get into films in the first place, Mr Gommershall? I'd *adore* to hear about it.'

Guy Gommershall flashed a wide smile, as if this was a story he loved telling. 'The War, you know. Reconnaissance. I flew over enemy lines and took photographs. When I wasn't being blasted out of the air by the Hun!'

He laughed again. Ella wondered how the War could possibly be amusing.

'After that I spent a while in California. Worked with the best—Fairbanks, Pickford, don't you know—'til I decided to bring some of that magic back home.'

Ella had no idea who he meant, but then she'd never been to the cinema. Mrs Prebble went sometimes; she'd have to ask her.

'You'll see,' Mr Gommershall went on. 'Film is going

to be the most important art form of the twentieth century. In twenty years' time you'll remember what I said!'

'You really can't beat a good book,' murmured Professor Otter.

'The smart people are investing now,' Guy Gommershall told them. He stooped even nearer and murmured to the professor. 'Connie and I are having a little tête-a-tête after this with people who want to get in on the game. Do stay. It's just a select few, you understand. Once the others are out of the way.'

He waved a casual hand at the vicar and his wife who stood nearby, gazing sadly at the tea table which looked as if a flock of starving birds had raided it.

Professor Otter consulted his watch and said, 'I'm afraid Ella here has a flute lesson in five minutes, and I'm expecting a visitor on a most—ah—pressing matter.' He went into a flurry of coughing and had to search in every one of his pockets for a handkerchief.

'Father—you told a lie,' Ella said, as they arrived at their own front door. 'Two lies, I think. My flute lesson isn't until tomorrow. And I'm sure no one is due to call this evening.'

Professor Otter smiled. 'A white lie, Ella, to be exact. There is a difference. I told a white lie because I didn't want to hurt Mr Gommershall's feelings. I wanted to go home and I don't want to get mixed up in anything to do with moving pictures.'

'Two white lies, then. To be exactly exact.'

They opened the door and Bernard slithered out and round their ankles. He sniffed disapprovingly at Ella's shoes. He could smell dog.

'What did that extraordinary fellow say?' the professor muttered, patting a pile of books with a loving hand. 'Film – the foremost art form of the twentieth century? What utter nonsense!'

Ella watched him trot off into his study. Then she dashed upstairs to her own room. She had so much to think about, and she needed to make urgent notes.

37 THE SHACKS

Quentin was a free agent. Mr and Mrs Cheeseman were out at a tea party to which children, thankfully, were not invited. They wouldn't be back for hours. He decided to go exploring.

He knew there was a footpath to the sea somewhere and found something promising at the end of the Finches' property. It wound round the backs of other people's gardens and on to a golf course. At last, puffing a bit, he reached the cliff path. The English Channel stretched out before him. A signpost pointed left to Seabourne, right to Oxcoombe. Seabourne and its spindly pier looked far off, faint and hazy. Oxcoombe looked nearer, and the route was downhill. He decided to go that way.

He tried not to get too close to the cliff-edge or look down. It made his knees feel like jelly. Even in his lightweight jumble-sale shirt and shorts, he was boiling hot and very thirsty. Spikes of thistle scratched his legs. He was pretty sure something had bitten him, too. He must be halfway to Oxcoombe by now—but it still looked very far away. Just a cluster of cottages round a church spire: it probably didn't even have an ice-cream stand! Once he got there he'd have to turn round and come back, all for nothing.

He found a sort of path going inland, little more than a wavering line through the thistles. He'd risk it and cut back to The Green. As long as he kept his bearings he couldn't get utterly lost. *Swamp or desert, jungle or barren plain, there was no territory that Horsefield could not find his way through.*

Up ahead were a couple of houses—shacks, really—he could ask someone there for a drink of water. As long as they weren't rough types, he thought, noticing how very run-down and ramshackle the places looked. He hoped there wouldn't be any snarling snapping dogs.

He approached the black-painted shack. It looked slightly more respectable than the other one, which was a patchwork of boards and slats and rusting sheets of corrugated iron. There was no sound or sign of life. But no dogs, either.

'Hello? I say!' he called. His voice came out more weak and wavery than he would have liked. 'Is anyone in? I simply want a glass of water, if I may.'

The empty windows stared at him. The door stayed shut.

Quentin jumped when a voice behind him said, 'He's out.'

He jumped again when he turned and saw who was speaking. There was a man in the rickety porch of the second shack. He kept to the shadows but Quentin could see that his face was badly scarred. Then the rough red skin broke apart and Quentin realized that the man was grinning.

'Apologies. It's rather a frightening face, isn't it? That's why I tend to keep out of everyone's way.'

'I—I—no—it's . . .' Quentin struggled to find the right thing to say. He wanted to say that of course he, Quentin, wasn't frightened, or that the face wasn't scary at all, or that the man didn't need to apologize, or all of those things, but of course they didn't come out. Because actually he was a bit scared and seeing a terribly damaged face so suddenly like that had been a bit of a shock.

'I can fetch you a glass of water if that's all you want. Or had you come to see Gommershall?'

'Who?' Quentin shook his head, then nodded. 'Um—no—er—yes. That would be very kind,' he managed to say. The man wasn't a ruffian, of that he was sure. His accent wasn't a ruffian's, for one thing. He sounded just like Daddy and Mr Cheeseman. When he came back with the water Quentin had a little speech prepared. 'I was walking along the cliffs when I realized that I'd been out a long time and ought to get home. I took a short cut—didn't mean to trespass at all. I was just very thirsty and hoped to get a drink.'

'That's all right, old chap.'

The man wore dirty overalls, an oily rag hanging from one pocket. His fingers were stained dark with grease and grime. Quentin stood on the yellowing grass in front of the shack, self-consciously drinking his water. *Horsefield drained the very last drop of reviving brandy while his rescuer stood watching. But was the man a friend—or a deadly foe?*

He finished and handed the glass back. 'Thank you.' A pause. Now or never. 'May I—may I ask—is it all right if I—?' He couldn't say it.

'Ask how I got like this? Flying. I flew reconnaissance in the War. Dipping over enemy lines, taking photographs. That's how they made the maps, you know. How they knew where to point the big guns. Of course those old planes are just paper and string and glue. When they get hit they go up like kindling, ablaze in moments. That's my story. More or less.'

A hero. A war hero. A flying ace.

Quentin blurted out, 'You know there's an airfield near here, don't you?' Mr Cheeseman still hadn't got round to taking him.

'I do indeed. The name's Atwood, by the way. Reggie Atwood.'

'John Horsefield,' said Quentin, carelessly, and shook the outstretched hand. 'I don't suppose you ever . . . not now . . . not with your . . .'

Reggie Atwood grinned again. 'Oh, I'm still in love with planes, if that's what you mean. Can't help it. You'll probably find me at the airfield, if you're ever there.' He nodded across at the other shack. 'I've been teaching my neighbour over the way how to fly—he's pretty good now, old Guy. Took to it like a natural.'

Flying lessons! thought Quentin. Perhaps Reggie Atwood would teach him, too. He wondered what his parents would say to that. They owed him a treat after his summer of all work and no fun.

'I do—I will—I mean, I'll be sure to visit the airfield very soon. Really ought to be off now. Thank you again.'

'Welcome, old chap. Follow this track 'til you get to the lane, then turn right and where it bends you'll see another path. That'll get you to The Green in no time. Hope your mother won't be worried.'

'Oh, she won't be!' Quentin said confidently, and with a wave, strode away.

Horsefield made successful contact with Agent X, who was hiding out at a remote location. Mission accomplished.

38 HUSBAND NO. 3?

NANCY'S JOURNAL

Well, that's the big tea-party over! My feet ache like fury and so does my head. I <u>wish</u> someone would let me have a lie-down & bring me a headache powder & a nice cup of tea.

Professor Otter came after all. Ella was wrong about him taking no notice of invitations. I must say he hadn't made much effort. Patches on his jacket elbows & the knot of his tie all sideways as if someone had just tried to strangle him. Ella was the smartest I've ever seen her—in velvet party slippers—& she'd combed her hair! But she managed to break a photo frame & now she's more interested in Mrs Bryce than what Cook's DARK DEEDS might be.

I showed the broken frame to Mrs Bryce and she did not seem one bit worried. So I put poor Mr Bryce to one side in the kitchen to await further orders & Cook said 'Take that out of the way before you get broken glass in the food!'

(More evidence that Cook hates husbands.) (Or hated Mr Bryce.) (Or that this photo isn't a preshus one of Mr Bryce AT ALL!)

What bothered me most at the party was:—

Which of the gentlemen was Mrs Bryce lining up as Husband No. 3?

I'm <u>sure</u> this is what she's up to. She lives beyond her means. I've seen the evidence: all this extrav-a-gance &

the piles of unpaid bills. So she hopes to catch a RICH HUSBAND. She's got to.

From what I could see Mrs B. was throwing herself at Prof. Otter. I'm afraid he may be TOP OF HER LIST. (Tho she also sat with Major Corcoran for ages & he looked pretty pleased at that.)

As to the rest of them—nobody called Mr Avery-Atkins arrived—nor did Timothy Finch. Alfred says the Finches own half the seafront & old Mr Finch never does anything but work work work. Timothy is just learning the business but he'll be the boss one day. I told Alfred 'You are truly a Fountain of Knowledge!' But he reminded me that he's always lived here—and Timothy Finch plays for the same cricket team as him. So does Constable Towner. (What a SMALL WORLD this is after London.)

So—what if Mrs Bryce & Professor Otter were to marry? Ella would have a mother at long last. A modern mother who would certainly spruce up her clothes & have fun & take her to exciting places—not just ruins and 2nd hand bookshops. She might smarten up Professor Otter too!

But what if the plan is to bump him off?? Then Ella would have lost BOTH her parents in tragic circumstances. I cannot let that happen.

But I may not have to do ANYTHING DRASTIC, for the following reasons:

Prof O. did NOT look so thrilled to see Mrs Bryce. In fact he looked quite worried.

Judging by appearances he is not rich. (Gran says 'You

can't judge a book by its cover'—which has sometimes led me & Aunty Bee to scream with laughter because you can judge the books we read by their covers. They are FULL of GORE.)

But I did overhear him & GG talk of fortunes in America. So maybe he is one of those SECRET MILLION-AIRS who walk around looking quite ordinary.

(Now I am feeling all muddled up. When I am tired my brain is tired.)

> **Detectives should not have to wait on everyone while they are detecting & then clear up after they have gone!**
>
> (Nancy Parker's Theory of Detection No. 4)

A few of the ~~gets~~ guests did stay on after tea but Prof. Otter was not one of them. I thoght they were going to wind up the Gramophone & roll back the carpets & dance like last time but they just sat around talking with IMPORTANT FACES on. I didn't learn anything useful as I was sent away until it was time to 'Fetch The Coats, Nancy!'

39 INSIDE BUSINESS

NANCY'S JOURNAL

No sooner than we got the parties over than I'm run off my feet turning the Morning Room into an Office for GG. Out with the spindly chairs & the pictures of flowers! (All heaved up to the attic by yours truly.) And in with a steel lamp & a type-writer & heaven knows what else, all fetched by delivery van. Mrs Bryce was full of orders—half of which she changed her mind over! But GG just stood about with his hands in his pockets laughing.

Another thing that arrived was boxes of brand-new writing paper from a London stationers. It's got BLUE SKY MOTION PICTURES printed at the top! (I remember the name from Mrs Bryce's list.)

Just the sight of it made me feel sick with excitement.

Now there's framed photos of Film Stars hung on the wall & a picture of them making a film on the desk—just a crowd of people standing round with cameras & so forth. It looks a right muddle to me but it's still exciting to see the INSIDE BUSINESS. I will nip back later to take a closer peep.

There's even a real CAMERA here for making motion pictures. They call it a Cine-Camera—pronounced 'Sinny'. It's a big wooden box with a handle & a glass eye on a tall 3-legged stand. I am forbidden to touch it—even with something as light as a feather duster.

'In fact Nancy I don't think we need you in here dusting AT ALL' Mrs Bryce said in the end.

The cheek of it!! She will soon find out that rooms don't stay clean & tidy by themselves. It takes ELBOW GREASE—& sore hands—& bruised knees & knuckles to keep everything looking how she wants it.

But I mustn't complain because we have
a real
FILM MAKERS OFFICE
right here in the house!!!

(A future me . . .)

Just so long as Mrs Bryce doesn't suddenly marry someone & Cook doesn't find a way to bump him off which would spoil everything before I get MY BIG CHANCE.

LATER

I confess while Mrs Bryce & GG were eating dinner (the bit with the coffee & the brandy which always takes a good long while) I DID slip back in.

GG's own special pen which looks like shiny red marble was lying on the desk & I picked it up & tried it out on the Blue Sky notepaper. I couldn't help it! I've got the sheet of paper here & I'll hide it in this journal.

Life at Cliffe Lodge is VERY EXCITING at the moment!!! I am so glad I got this job and not another nearer home.

BLUE SKY MOTION PICTURES
14 Ember Place, Park Street, London W1.
Telephone Mayfair 307

I promise to make Miss Nancy Parker a famous film star!!!

Signed

Yours truly

Guy Gommershall

40 DIAGNOSIS BOREDOM

Professor Otter had diagnosed Holiday Boredom—just when Ella wasn't bored at all—and prescribed lots to occupy her—just when she was far too busy pursuing her studies in Anthropology and Psychology.

Which is why she found herself hurrying through the back streets of Seabourne, carrying her flute and her music case and list of topics to look up at the Public Library. She was on her way there after an extra flute lesson, and Father wanted to see—and hear—the results when she got home.

But she wasn't thinking about any of that. Her thoughts were full of Mrs Bryce and her artificial laugh and why she would choose to entertain the whole neighbourhood if she had to put on an act to do it. She had her head down and scarcely saw her own feet; which was why she blundered into a woman hurrying the other way, loaded with shopping. A bag full of potatoes swung at her legs, and a sharp elbow knocked her in the ribs.

'Watch where you're going, young lady!'

Ella swung round to make a face at the retreating back, and something caught her eye. The next-door shop had a sign saying:

Bodger & Son, Quality Furnishings & House Clearance.

The quality furnishings (grim wardrobes, saggy chairs) were in the window, but arranged on tables on the pavement were all manner of smaller things. It was a box that Ella had spotted—a box of old photos in tarnished frames.

She put down her music and her flute case and sorted through them. Ladies dressed in crinolines like Queen Victoria, gentlemen with huge beards and side-whiskers, grumpy children in fussy old-fashioned outfits. Weddings. Christenings. Soldiers in uniform. Some had handwritten messages, names and best wishes, scrawled across them. These photos were out on the pavement because B. Bodger & Son cleared houses when someone died and took away the junk that no one else wanted. Ella felt sad: these people posed so proudly for their photographs and nobody now remembered who they were.

Two lines of inky letters ran through her brain: *To dearest Lettie & little May, With love, Leonard xx.* It would be easy to fake a history! For just a few shillings she could buy herself a set of photographs, surround herself with grandfathers and cousins and long-ago parties. They might not look anything like her, but if she arranged them on the mantelpiece at home visitors would assume that they were family. She could tell everyone that they were Father's side, in distant America, and no one would suspect a thing! (Except Father and Mrs Prebble, of course, who would wonder what was going on.) Ella was almost tempted to try it out—an experiment in Psychology. And it would give her evidence—evidence enough to show that Mrs Bryce's family could be fake, too.

Because she had the strongest suspicion that those old pictures—the man in uniform, the elderly couple, the crowded wedding party—were simply bought off a stall like this one. The only genuine photos were the recent ones of Mrs Bryce herself.

'Can I help you, miss?'

It was Mr Bodger, or his son, standing in the doorway.

'Yes. What do people buy these for?'

'The frames, mostly.'

'Doesn't anyone want them for the pictures?'

'Now why would they do that?'

'If they knew the person, or . . .'

'If anyone still knew the party involved they wouldn't be stuck out here. It's not very dignified, is it? Now, are you buying, or not?'

Ella thumbed through again until she came to the one she just couldn't leave behind: a battered frame no wider than her hand, enclosing a small child hugging a large dog.

'How much?'

'Sixpence, that one. You fond of dogs?'

Ella nodded and handed over her money. She did like dogs, but Mrs Prebble disapproved of them in the house—even tiny, neat ones like Sausage—and Bernard disapproved of them on principle.

Forgetting all about the library, Ella pocketed the photograph. She wanted to get back and show it to Nancy.

41 MIDNIGHT MERMAID

NANCY'S JOURNAL

We've had a stream of visitors since GG set up his office here. I must say that when I announce them GG never decides he is NOT AT HOME!

But no visitors this morning—'cos Mrs Bryce & GG were off out for the day. On important FILM BUSINESS I expect. And I ended up being sent on a very strange errand. I'd just picked up Mrs Bryce's breakfast tray when she said 'Nancy! You're about the same size as me.' She threw a frock at me (her silver snake one) & told me to 'PUT IT ON.'

I must say I have never worn anything like it—so light and easy it just slithered over my head. Mrs Bryce must wear a different kind of petticoat from mine. (Well, I know she does—I'm tidying them up all the time!) Mine made great lumps & bumps under that slinky silk frock. Even so I would say I was the nearest to ELEGANT that I've ever been!

Then she made me turn round and round to show how I looked. But she wasn't looking at me. She was looking at the frock to see how it fitted. 'You'll do a treat' she said.

'Cos Mrs Bryce had clean forgot about a dressmakers fitting—and SIMPLY COULDN'T be in 2 PLACES AT ONCE!! Her new frock was almost ready, only needed the hem measuring. She said 'Those heels of yours are the same height as my silver Evening Slippers. Make sure you wear those shoes when you go.' (As if I had 100 different pairs to choose from!)

So that was how I ended up spending the afternoon at the Dressmakers—balanced on a table with pins sticking in me.

Alfred drove me into Seabourne & along the High Street which is full of smart shops. I expected the dressmakers to be here but Alfred carried on right to the Railway Station & stopped in a lane round the back. It was just a plain little house with a sooty hedge and red ~~Germ~~ Geraniums by the door.

The dressmaker—name of Mrs Lockett—was about Aunty Bee's age. Very thin, in a plain black dress with a velvet pin-cushion tied to her wrist & a tape-measure round her neck. She looked put out to see me at first and then sort of—releeved.

'You won't mind standing on the table, will you?' she said. 'I can't ask MY LADIES to stand up there while I pin their hems—that would not be POLITE—but I <u>do</u> find this job is hard on my knees.'

We were in her front room. Two little kiddies kept peeping round the door & giggling. I don't suppose they are allowed to do that when HER LADIES are there. I could not resist making funny faces every time they peeped in—which just made them worse. When she saw this Mrs Lockett fell into chatting. After a time she said 'Call me Maisie' & she made us a cup of tea.

She tacked up the hem while I sat & did nothing. (What a treat!) We were such chums by then I felt I could say how I had pictured Mrs Bryce getting her clothes made somewhere much more grand. (Tho I tried not to make this sound insulting.)

'Oh, no, then she'd have to pay FAR MORE!' said Mrs Lockett (Maisie). 'Not that she's much good at paying at all.' Then she clutched her mouth as if she had said too much.

I don't wish to be disloyal to Mrs Bryce, but I could have said I knew that all too well. There was an UNPAID dressmakers bill of £20 in that wooden box in the Morning Room. Yet here I was back to collect another frock.

(There were bills for Champagne & for printing Calling Cards too. It makes me go all hot to think how much Mrs Bryce spends on such silly things.)

(Or—more like—feels free to order & not pay for.)

'Why do you let them get away with it?' I asked—trying to make it sound like a general comment.

Maisie said 'What can I do? It's worth it to have someone like your Mrs Bryce as a customer—even if she NEVER gets round to paying. Such a lovely figure, so elegant, so up-to-date! All the other ladies want to copy her style & so they come to me. They can't get looks like that in our dull old High Street—and they won't pay high London prices.'

If Maisie Lockett was Seabourne's best-kept fashun secret I wanted to know how did Mrs Bryce, a stranger, find her? Through Mrs Avery-Atkins apparently—the Lady Mayoress—she could always sniff out a bargain.

(That name rang a bell! It's on Mrs Bryce's HUSBAND LIST.)

(But if Mr Avery-Atkins already has a wife it can't be a list of Possible Husbands.)

Then she cut the end off her thread & made me try the frock on again. It is a beautifull midnight-blue silk with a kind of wrinkle like waves in the sea—but a wrinkle that is meant to be there. Mrs Bryce will look like a slippery MIDNIGHT MERMAID in it!

Now Maisie seemed to think there was something wrong with the neck. She made me lift my hair out of the way. All the frizzy bits kept flying out, what with trying-on clothes all day. (The best way to make my hair behave is not to touch it.) (Ever.)

Maisie said I should get it cut off into a bob like Mrs Bryce. That it would suit me & be easy to keep tidy. She said all sorts of nice things about my hair which I will not put down here. Her sister Louie—who shares their house—is a Hairdresser and will do it for me!

I did say my only time off was Sundays (tho Sundays off is another thing Mrs Bryce has not been good about) and besides I am a bit short of funds.

'I'm sure Louie will cut it for free' Maisie said 'since YOU ARE A FREND.'

I came away with such a glow. I had forgotten how much I missed just chatting & being frendly in an ordinary little parlour with people who are Good and Kind. Now I am DETERMINED to get Mrs Bryce to coff up for Maisie's bills. I swear I will find a way!!

42 SCRAMBLED

Quentin's scrambled egg was fluffy and deep, deep yellow. It looked nothing like the heaps of pale watery stuff they served up for breakfast at school.

'About that jumble, Quentin . . .' Mrs Cheeseman began.

He couldn't think what she meant. Mrs Cheeseman had washed and ironed the blue summer shirt he'd got from the jumble box and sewn on a button to replace one that was missing. She'd even conjured up a similar shirt, in yellow. He was wearing it today. Was that what she was on about? He loaded a piece of toast with more egg and bit into it.

Mrs Cheeseman went on, 'Yesterday evening Miss Dearing and I, on behalf of the Jumble Sale Committee, went through everything that has been collected.'

Quentin went hot and then instantly cold. The toast felt like cardboard in his mouth. Soggy cardboard. He understood what she meant now. She knew. She knew about the stolen goods, she *knew* it was him who'd put them there.

'Quentin.' Her voice sounded firm, as firm as when she was dealing with unwanted visitors. 'I know you took an interest in the vestry jumble box.' She seemed to be waiting for an answer.

John Horsefield would never be broken under interrogation.

Quentin mumbled, 'Errff.'

'Miss Dearing is convinced—'

Of course she was. It was probably Miss Dearing who stole the blasted stuff in the first place. Of course she would want to switch the suspicion to someone else.

'—but I myself am not sure . . .'

Quentin kept his head down. The rest of his egg grew solid on the plate.

'You see, we found some small items of value. Just the same as those that Jim—that Constable Towner—told us had been stolen from houses round The Green.' She paused again, waiting for him.

Quentin murmured, 'Ummph?'

'Items stolen in just the last few weeks. Did you know anything about this, Quentin?'

Quentin gurgled, 'Nnngg.'

'There was certainly nothing strange in the jumble box last time I looked in it. So it can only have been after that . . . Quentin? Quentin!'

All he could do was shake his head.

Mrs Cheeseman's voice grew softer, baffled. 'I'm sure they weren't there last week. I keep telling myself I wouldn't have missed them. Last week it was all cast-off clothes and odd balls of wool. I wondered if you saw anything valuable, Quentin, when you were rummaging about?'

She didn't know. She didn't know anything—and nor did Miss Dearing! Quentin shoved his chair back and stood up.

'Well . . . it's quite a mystery! Miss Dearing seemed very

relieved when I said that I would mention it to the vicar and that he would speak to Constable Towner about it. Oh—is there something wrong with your egg? Is everything all right?'

He shook his head vigorously. 'Honestly, Mrs Cheese, it was delish. Honestly, I never saw anything in that box but jumble. Honestly.'

He headed for the door, as fast as his shaking legs would carry him.

Mrs Cheeseman wiped her hands on a dish-towel. She called after him, 'I'm sorry, Quentin. I didn't mean to imply that there's anything wrong with wearing cast-off clothes.'

43 VANISHED DREAMS

NANCY'S JOURNAL

Oh dear! Mrs Bryce's good mood of the last few days is gone. Quite vanished!!

I wonder if it is to do with Husband Hunting. Maybe it isn't working out how she planned.

I could tell just by the way she pressed the bell that she was cross. It carried on much longer & louder than usual. My heart was in my boots (not that I am wearing boots) as I went in. What had I done wrong now?

Turns out it was: —

I broke 2 plates (True but a long time ago) (So no one has ever spotted the chipped gravy boat!)

I get more post than a housemaid should!!!

I've been seen gossiping on The Green (?)

So Cook has been gossiping to her.

Mrs Bryce seems most put out about the post. I said I had been forced to move FAR FROM MY FAMILY & it was only natural they sent me their news & a few books from time to time. I almost forgot to say M'm afterwards—cos I was feeling so cross myself.

I <u>hope</u> Cook hasn't steamed open any of my letters and read them. She has enough STEAM at her disposal what with boiling pans & kettles. Tho how could she inter-sept them? It is always me who fetches the post from the doormat. That's how I know Cook doesn't get any.

Next Mrs Bryce said—with her mouth all screwed up tight 'You gave me to beleeve you had no family.'

'No I did not!' (I think I DID forget the M'm that time.)

The only time we spoke of them was when Mrs Bryce engaged me & then I told her about my Dad—and that I had no mother. We never got as far as Aunty Bee & Gran. She never ASKED. Or I would have said.

'You have been deceeving me Nancy!' she said, even more prune-faced.

'No I have not—M'm—I would not.' I explained that it was only Aunty Bee who wrote and that she read out my letters to the other two. Next Mrs Bryce wanted to know what I wrote to them about—which I thought was going TOO FAR.

Then 'Nancy—you know what I said about being RELIABLE and DISCREET. Gossiping with neighbours is hardly Discreet!'

I don't see how Cook could have seen me as she is always round the back of the house & busy. Unless Mrs Bryce has got others spying for her? Not Alfred surely? I can't beleve Alfred would side against me.

'You are going to have to watch your step' she said. (Exactly what Cook said about those plates.) 'If I hear anything of this again—ANYTHING—you will be looking for another place. And don't think tears can sway me.'

(That was just her imagination.) (If my eyes were watering it was due to RAGE.)

It is so unfair that she can have her say—and I must

just stand there and take it. I dare not answer back. Not if I want to keep my job or get a good reckommendation off her for the next one.

But she cannot sack me just now—they have another party coming up. A dinner for all the people who want to be in GG's film. They need me on hand to spill the sauce into ladies laps and drop potatoes into gentlemens wineglasses! I suppose they could hire another maid to do it. Or that flashy waiter from Seabourne with the satin waistcoat. (I bet he never drops a thing.)

I always felt Mrs Bryce was kind & nice but now I think I have been misled. I may have been swayed by her looks & her easy manner about some things. I may have been IMPRESSED. Because she is not like anyone else I ever came across before. And because she can be nice when she wants to. When she puts it on.

Ella was right on that score—she spotted it much quicker than I did. One whiff of Mrs Bryce close-to at the party & she saw she was faking things. (Faking what, I'm still not sure.)

I must say my chances of being in one of GG's films—even just as an extra in a crowd scene—seem very far away now. I will just have to become a Detective instead!! Tho right now I feel DOOMED to be a housemaid all my days.

I just took out GG's little note with the air-o-plane on it to cheer myself up. It did make me smile. Then I looked at the Blue Sky headed paper to read what I wrote again.

What I found there made me even MORE downcast. My words have vanished! It's as if I never put that little joke to myself—as if even MY DREAMS never happened.

I am not going to write any more in here tonight.

44 Bread Street,
London.

Dear Nancy,
Just a quick letter (I am writing this in my dinner break at the
Depot) to say we haven't heard from you in a while. I hope
everything is all right. I expect you are very busy. You are not
ill, are you? You WOULD let us know if you were? I am
sure the sea breezes are keeping you well & you're just rushed
off your feet. Like me!! (This hot weather doesn't help. My
feet are prize-winning marrows by the time I get home.)
Do write soon, Nancy, as Grandma and your Dad cannot
help worrying about you, so far away. You would tell us if
there was anything wrong, wouldn't you? Be a sensible girl.
Love from everyone here (I do not mean in the bus depot!!)

Aunty Bee xxx

44 A MODERN GIRL

NANCY'S JOURNAL

My afternoon off & the sun was shining! I hopped on The Valiant & rode into Seabourne by way of the lanes. I did not come to greef at all. Tho I must admit I may wobble when a motor-car goes dashing past. I found my way to Maisie Lockett's house with hardly any mistakes. She was home with the 2 little boys and so was her sister Louie.

I sat there in fear & trembling while Louie's ~~scis~~ sissors snipped all round my head. (I had my eyes shut!) Maisie kept saying 'It will suit you'—& 'It will be so much less bother'—and kind things like that. But now it was really happening I worried I would end up looking a FRIGHT.

A FRIGHT

A MODERN GIRL

But I don't. I am a Modern Girl with neat bobbed hair! Not sleek & shiny like Mrs Bryce's bob. Sort of high and bouncy—that's because of the Natural Curl, Louie says. (And she added I am not to call it FRIZZ.)

Louie said that with her in HAIRDRESSING and Maisie in DRESSMAKING they are bound to hear the latest gossip from all the Ladies who come in. Except she called it NEWS.

So I asked them about Husband-hunting. Louie said 'Women have to be clever these days because husbands are so thin on the ground.' Then Maisie said 'Not thin but fat—and old and ugly to boot!' They think it a great joke.

We had a cup of tea & bread & butter & ham & tomatoes. I could see they had to stretch it a bit cos I was there. I really wanted to pay for my haircut but Louie wouldn't hear of it. Maisie just laughed. 'If your Mrs Bryce doesn't trouble herself about anything so vulgar as money—I don't see why her housemaid should!!'

(So I knew then that her bill was still UNPAID.)

Louie said 'I wonder if she will want her hair trimming soon? You can put in a good word for me, can't you, Nancy!'

I don't know how they can find it so funny.

Since we were on such good terms I asked if they'd heard any NEWS about Mrs Bryce & a possible husband. Maisie said 'I'm sure she could find one if she wanted. She's got herself invited to all the grandest places.' And then Louie added she was after their money without having to marry anyone—she wants them to pay for the film that her friend was making.

'Mr Gommershall?' I asked. 'Oh the Mystery Man!' said Louie. 'No one knows much about him—except he's got chums who are famous Film Stars. Or so he says!'

185

I told them I thoght everyone in Seabourne wanted to BE in the film. Louie shrieked at that. 'Guy Gommershall only wants their MONEY. Not their ugly mugs filling up the screen! And Mrs Bryce is very good at sweet-talking rich people. Anyone with any cash is mad to give it to them.' That's what Louie said, anyway.

(By mad I thoght that she meant KEEN. Now I wonder if she means CRAZY?) Except—if GG hasn't got a bean either—maybe that's why he's staying in that Shack. Waiting for the film money to flow in.

I must say I found it a releef to hear that Mrs Bryce doesn't want to marry—& Maisie & Louie are likely to know, if anyone does. Now I can stop worrying about Cook murdering Professor Otter. Or anyone else for that matter.

(Tho it does dash my latest Theory somewhat!)

But I must have felt carefree for I didn't think of them again until I was back at Cliffe Lodge.

As I rode home I could feel the breeze around my neck. It was most ~~discons~~ ~~dissconsett~~ disconcerting. But also LIGHT and PLEASANT and COOL.

Just as I put the Valiant away I saw the motor-car approaching—with Mrs Bryce at the wheel! Alfred was sitting beside her. After she got out & went indoors he parked the car carefully himself. I went over & said 'I didn't know Mrs Bryce could drive a car.' (I was hoping that Alfred would notice I looked different but he didn't remark on it at all.)

He has been TEACHING HER. He said 'You know what

186

she is like. She can charm you into anything when she wants to.' His uncle would not be pleased if he knew—the car is very valuable. Alfred only let her take the wheel in some quiet corner and never on the roads. The quiet corner is an Airfield—where the air-o-plane with the banner flies from. There is plenty of room & nobody to see them or crash into.

But she was ON THE ROADS just now!

He said 'Becos she ignored my instrucktions & drove off before I could stop her. When I told it wasn't safe she just laughed.'

I have never seen Alfred in a BAD MOOD before. Or heard him say a BAD WORD about anyone. Not that it was a bad word—he just gave me to understand that Mrs Bryce does whatever she wants & blow the ~~conseck~~ consie-quences! Which is true.

No wonder he never noticed my new hair.

Post Card

Dear All,

Just to let you know I am now a thoroghly Modern Girl. I have BOBBED MY HAIR and I go about on A BIKE! Aunty Bee—you would be proud. Hope Dad & Gran approve. The sun is shining & the beach is crowded with trippers. Wish you were here.

All my love,
Nancy x

45 ADVICE FROM AN EXPERT

Ella Otter sat in her bedroom, surrounded by brown paper and string. And school uniform. She was in a bad mood.

It was still early August. School didn't start until September. September seemed a nice, safe, long way away. Except that it was creeping closer with every moment, and even though Ella tried not to let this thought enter her mind at all, it had entered her stomach and gave her a nervous sort of ache.

Early August was when Mrs Prebble took her annual holiday. She went to stay with her sister in Kent. Last year Ella had joined her father on an archaeological dig. It was great fun. She slept in a tent in a field for a fortnight, and ate sausages cooked, or more like *burnt*, over an open fire. The year before there had been no dig—it was still wartime—but it was fun anyway. (Ella realized now that you weren't supposed to have fun in wartime—but she'd only been nine then, and nine-year-olds, she told herself, didn't really know anything.) She and her father lived on sandwiches and things out of cans and often picnicked on the study floor or ate round a bonfire in the garden so late that darkness was falling and the moon stood high above the house. Ella hardly washed and no one asked her to put on a clean frock or brush her hair. She brushed her teeth of her own accord because she didn't like the stale taste of baked beans or sardine sandwiches in her mouth. This summer, however, there was no dig, and her father was writing a book, so she didn't think there would be much in the way of picnicking or bonfires.

And Mrs Prebble had given Ella an ultimatum. They needed to get her uniform for grammar school. They could buy it when Mrs Prebble returned from Kent— though there might be nothing left by then, or only items in all the wrong sizes—or they could buy it before she went away.

Ella knew what the correct answer was. She really really didn't want to go and try on blazers and hats and tunics, or even think about them before she had to, but neither did she want to turn up on her first day at school—her first day at any proper school ever—in an outsize blazer and a tiny hat! So, with a groan that turned into a sigh, she agreed with Mrs Prebble that the wisest course was to visit the school outfitters right away.

Which was why she now sat on the bedroom floor with about ten unpacked parcels of hideous school clothing all about her. Brown and yellow and maroon: the ugliest colours put together in the sickliest combinations. A brown tunic, a yellow sash. A yellow and maroon tie. A brown hat with a yellow and maroon hatband! A stiff serge blazer with a glaring badge on the pocket!! There was even a hockey stick. (She had no idea how to play hockey but apparently you needed this weapon.) Why had she ever let her father persuade her that school would be a good idea?! It was a hateful idea, and a hateful uniform. And the place would be stuffed with hateful girls. Girls who all knew each other, and knew their way around. (And how to play hockey!)

She glared at the hat, and then threw it across the room. Mrs Prebble was already on the train to Kent. She had left a glazed pork pie, cold potatoes and a washed lettuce in the pantry. There were raspberries and cream for pudding. After that they would fend for themselves. But Professor Otter was happily tucked away in his study with a towering pile of notes and ten new bottles of ink. Ella recalled with longing the tent in the field and the burnt sausages, and wondered if it was worth running away.

Instead she got up, aimed a kick at the hat—which lay upside-down in the doorway—and went downstairs. She was going to take matters into her own hands. She would go and see an expert.

Quentin thought he was safely out of sight in the complicated boughs of the cedar tree when he saw That Girl come kicking her way across the churchyard.

Yet, without even raising her eyes, she bellowed, 'I know you're up there, Quentin Ives!'

The next surprise was, 'Can I come up there, too? I want to ask you something.'

Quentin kept quiet.

'It's about something you're an expert in.'

Well, thought Quentin, and ran through a number of things she might be referring to. Except that he couldn't come up with anything. Not really. Unless it was about Top Secret stuff. Carrying out heroic missions, and suchlike.

'School!' she shouted. 'It's about school.'

Before he could answer, there were the unmistakable sounds of someone scrabbling up the tree. She arrived at his branch more quickly than he expected.

'Pax, Quentin. I know that's something they say at school. I read it in a book. Let's call a Truce, eh?'

She stuck out a hand for him to shake. Quentin had to let go with one hand to shake back. He muttered, 'Pax,' and shuffled along the branch to make room.

Ella settled herself beside him. 'I s'pose I ought to thank you for secretly disposing of those stolen goods. I didn't realize at the time that it would get me off the hook. I thought you'd landed me in deeper trouble.'

'Did you hear what happened in the end?' Quentin said. 'Mrs Cheeseman found them in amongst the jumble and Mr Cheeseman put a notice in the Parish News thanking everyone for their generous donations.'

Ella laughed so hard at this that she nearly shook them both off the branch.

Once they were steady again Quentin said, rather casually, 'Now, you wanted my expert advice?'

'Yes. You know all about school, don't you? I don't mean how to do the lessons—they won't be difficult for me, and I know you're a duffer in that respect. I mean school in general.'

Quentin prickled at this insult. On the other hand,

he felt quite proud that she believed he knew the other stuff. 'What kind of things?'

'People. Games. Making friends.'

'Ah.'

'I know you go to boarding school, and mine is only a day school, so I don't need to find out about dormitories and midnight feasts and stuff like that. Although midnight feasts do sound like fun.'

They might be fun, Quentin thought, if anyone had ever included him in them.

'The trouble is,' Ella went on, 'Father isn't much interested in games, and nor am I, so I haven't got a clue how you play them. I've got to do hockey—I've even got the stick—but I've no idea what you do with it. I expect I shall be a complete duffer when it comes to games. But I know you're very keen. I've heard you and Mr Cheeseman playing cricket in the vicarage garden.'

'Well,' said Quentin, relaxing now, and feeling that indeed he was a bit of an expert in how a duffer dealt with games. He leaned back—unwise when sitting on a branch—and quickly had to adjust his position. 'What I'd advise is, get in a bit of practice first . . .'

46 ELLA'S INSTINCTS

It was hot and sticky and there was a low roar like far-off thunder in the air; or it might just be the aeroplane with the banner. Ella was ready to go home. The conversation about school had been very useful and she was feeling much more optimistic.

But as they clambered down out of the cedar tree, Quentin said, 'I thought you'd come to ask for help with a secret mission. I've done a few myself now, and I know this chap who's a real war hero . . .'

Ella hesitated. 'Secret missions? Is that what you're up to? I've seen you nosing about. You're not half as careful as you think, you know.'

Quentin turned away and stumped off in the direction of the vicarage.

'Wait!' Ella shouted. 'Pax!! Double pax, or whatever they say.'

He stopped, but didn't turn.

'I could do with some help.'

He spun round.

'What do you know about the people at Cliffe Lodge?'

'Cliffe Lodge?'

'The house next-door to mine. Not the pink castle, the redbrick villa. Connie Bryce and Guy Gommershall.

Or GG, as she calls him.'

'Gommershall . . . that sounds familiar.'

'Really? Think!' Ella sat down on her usual tombstone and glared at Quentin. 'I need to know. Even if it seems unimportant—'

'—Because the smallest thing may turn out to be the most important.'

'Yesss!' Ella could see that his mind ran along similar lines to hers.

Quentin asked, 'Is he the Gommershall who lives at those tumbledown shacks? It's a remote sort of place. Reggie Atwood—my war hero—lives there. He was terribly injured, you see, as an air ace, and doesn't like to be where everyone can stare at him.'

'A tumbledown shack! Hardly. GG is a movie magnate.'

'What's that?'

'Something important to do with films.'

'Oh, yes. The Cheesemans were very excited when they came back from Mrs Bryce's tea party. A film's going to be made right here in Seabourne and everyone seems to think they'll be in it. Mrs Cheeseman was hurt that they weren't asked to stay on after tea. She wasn't one of the chosen few, she kept saying. Unlike the Finches.'

Ella said, 'If you were going to choose someone to star in your next film, would it be Mrs Cheeseman— who looks like a camel? Or would it be Penny or Popsy Finch? They're as silly as chickens but they do have pretty faces.'

Looking down at his shoes, Quentin concentrated on kicking a stone. Ella thought he was trying not to laugh, or to show her that she could make him laugh.

'It wasn't about that,' he said after a bit. 'Mrs Cheeseman was hurt because they haven't any money to spare, and this GG chap is only interested in people who can invest.'

'Invest?'

'Put their money into GG's film company. Then when it's a roaring success and makes a bundle of profit, they'll get even more money back.'

Ella clasped her knees and rocked back and forth, which always helped her think. 'What happens,' she said slowly, 'if the film is a flop?'

Quentin shrugged. 'They lose all their money, I suppose. Investment is always a risk. That's what Daddy says, anyhow.'

'What if they can't afford to lose their money? Sounds to me as if Mrs Cheeseman is lucky to be out of it.'

'That's not what she thinks.' Quentin kicked his stone right round the tomb. 'You know, I swear Guy Gommershall was the name Reggie Atwood mentioned. He asked if I'd come to see Gommershall and pointed to the other shack.'

'It seems odd that someone like GG would live somewhere like that. Unless he doesn't want people to find him.'

'And Mr Atwood said he was teaching old Guy to fly . . .'

Ella frowned. 'But Guy Gommershall already knows how. I heard him tell Father he flew reconnaissance planes.'

'No! That's what my war hero did! He flew over enemy lines so they could take pictures and spy out the land. But it was a frightfully risky business and he got shot down and burnt.'

Ella jumped off the tomb. She grabbed Quentin by his arm. 'I think Guy Gommershall has stolen another man's story and is passing it off as his own! He boasted that he flew planes in the war. That he took pictures. Is he boastful, your war hero?'

'No. Not at all. He only told me all that because—because I asked about his face. It's pretty ugly to look at.'

'GG's not ugly to look at. People seem to think the opposite. And he dresses in a way that makes everyone notice. Baggy white trousers and red stripy blazers!'

Quentin looked as if he had swallowed a fly. 'Red blazers? If that's Guy Gommershall, then I've met him. I showed him round the church.'

'What for?'

'Because I happen to know a lot about it,' Quentin said. 'He was interested in tombs and memorials and things. Who the rich old families were. Why do you want to know all this, anyhow?'

Ella stared Quentin in the eye. 'According to my observations, Mrs Bryce and Guy Gommershall are both utter fakes and liars! Always sneaking and snooping and sweet-talking people. I'm sure she's pretending to be something—or someone—that she isn't. Now it seems he's doing the same. All my instincts tell me they must be up to something very bad.'

Quentin stared back. 'Your instincts? Up to what? Do you have any proof?'

Ella blinked. 'Not yet. But I will. I will.'

47 A FUNNY FEELING

NANCY'S JOURNAL

I must quickly put this down on paper. I haven't got a Theory—no time for that!—this is just My Observations.

But SOMETHING IS UP.

The pantry shelves are half bare. They are usually groaning when we have a party coming up. I <u>know</u> there's been a bit of trouble with deliveries. Cook had to find another Butcher after that row she had over the steak. Those UNPAID BILLS cannot have helped.

I came up the stairs to my room earlier—the door to the attic was open & I saw Mrs Bryce inside. I slipped out of the way & she went downstairs with her big suitcase. She didn't ask me to fetch it. Or pack it—& <u>usually</u> she is full of orders.

Now her wardrobe is almost empty. I cannot bring myself to beleve that she's selling her lovely dresses to raise some cash. Not when she just ordered that new frock from Maisie Lockett.

There's a funny feeling in the house. Can't put my finger on it. The weather's hot & heavy but it isn't just that. They may not be planning Marriage and Murder any more but SOMETHING IS GOING ON.

It sort of reminds me of the time the Uptons next-door-but-one did a MIDNIGHT FLIT from Bread Street on account of not being able to pay the rent. I saw Mrs Upton tying everything up in a blanket—and quietly calling the kids in from the street—and next morning their house was empty. I never heard any cart or barrow creeping away in the dark—but then me & Aunty Bee sleep at the back.

(But Cliffe Lodge is as far from Bread Street as you can get.)

LATER

Now I know that Mrs Bryce is not short of cash cos I went into the Morning Room to dust & caught her—she was counting it into that Wooden Box she keeps on the writing desk. She was quick to close the lid & turn the key but I saw a stack of notes inside. I acted as if I had not—in fact I pretended to trip on the rug & got told off for being so clumsy. I would rather she thinks I'm CLUMSY than NOSEY.

Was this money from selling the frocks? Then Alfred said he had driven Mrs Bryce to the Bank that day. She went in a bit nervous & came out humming a tune so it must have gone well.

(Whatever it is people do in banks. This is not in my PERSONAL EXPERIENSE.)

(Get a load of money out, in her case.)

I no longer feel that Life Is So Exciting as I said a few pages back. The Blue Sky Motion Picture Company is underway so I should be over the moon that my big chance may truly come. Except the moon seems to have gone behind a cloud.

48 LAVINIA OTTER'S WINDOW

Ella was furious with Quentin Ives. Because she'd granted a Truce which he didn't really deserve. Because he dismissed her instincts and demanded proof. But most of all because he'd shown that nasty lying Guy Gommershall around the church, the church where her mother's own special memorial window was. It wasn't his window to show off to anyone, and she didn't want someone like Guy Gommershall gawping at it as if it was just an *object of interest*.

She and her father ate the supper Mrs Prebble had left in silence. Professor Otter didn't seem to notice anything wrong and kept his eyes on the book he was reading. Afterwards Ella washed the plates, banging them about so hard it was a wonder she didn't break anything. Her father made a pot of coffee for one and carried it off to his study.

Ella stood in the middle of the kitchen and glared at Bernard. Bernard gazed back, a look of utter innocence on his wide ginger face.

'I'm going out!' she said to no one in particular.

A great bank of cloud had turned the evening dark. The sky lit up with a sudden flash, followed by the distant growl of thunder. Instantly rain began to patter about her. Ella stamped her way across The Green, glad that she was getting soaked.

Despite the gloom she walked bravely through the churchyard. She could see lights in the vicarage windows. That Boy would be inside. She hoped he was struggling with a long list of vile Latin verbs, or page after page of the most intractable mathematic equations. She did not want to think of him loafing in an armchair with a pile of comics and gorging on Mrs Cheeseman's walnut cake.

She did not want to think of him at all.

She pushed open the door to the church. It was dimmer than ever inside. She wiped her feet and went up the central aisle as if on stepping stones. There were burial marker stones in the floor and she didn't like to tread on any of those. Especially the one with the skull carved into it.

A small light glowed near the altar. Her mother's window was to one side. Its glorious colours were nothing in the grey evening. They needed daylight behind them; best of all, the sun. *Lavinia Otter*, it said. *Bright as the dawn, brighter than the day.*

Ordinarily Ella didn't feel sad. She didn't miss a mother she'd never known. She felt proud of the beautiful window and of her father for putting it there, finding an artist who could make it full of light and life. But tonight, with Mrs Prebble—the nearest she had to a mother—far away, and Father sunk deep in his studies, Ella felt low. There was no one to listen to her troubles. Quentin Ives had proved helpful for a while, but then he'd turned back into *That Boy* again. She hadn't managed to catch Nancy for days, and anyway, Nancy's ideas clashed with her own. The girl seemed to like Mrs Bryce! She admired Guy Gommershall!!

Ella could hear the rain—heavy now—pounding on the church roof. The leaky gutter on the north side began to splash.

'Soon they'll see I'm right,' she said aloud, to Lavinia Otter's window. 'I'll show them! You see if I don't.'

Pausing in the doorway, she pulled her cardigan over her head. The churchyard didn't look like anyone's favourite place any more. Ghostly tombstones loomed out of the dark and the cedar tree draped sinister arms over everything.

Ella took a deep breath and dived out into the downpour.

A ghastly apparition rose up from the graves. Flapping palely, it clutched Ella to its cold wet flesh!

49 THE VERY WORST

NANCY'S JOURNAL

The VERY WORST has happened!

   I have been found out—and thrown out!!

   The WORST of THE WORST is that I've lost my Diary of Detection.

And everything in it!

   Mrs Bryce beleeves I stole twenty pounds (the £20 I was taking to make sure Maisie Lockett got paid) and some notepaper.

   It is <u>true</u> I stole paper & envelopes—& not just the sheet of Blue Sky Pictures she knows about. But then I'd had no wages & needed to write Home.

   She came in as I was getting Maisie's money from that Wooden Box. I had the key in one hand & four £5 notes in the other. There was still a stack of notes left but she says I would have <u>taken it all</u> if she hadn't found me when she did.

   She shouted for Cook & they marched me up to my room to search for anything else I had stolen—which they <u>knew</u> I must have. When I tried to explain they called me An Insolent Girl and A Theef.

   Mrs Bryce went straight to my books—she didn't seem to care much about the tattered old murder ones—but she leafed thru Sherlock Holmes & the Dictionary. 'Aha! There's more!!' she cried when she found Ella Otter's name in the Dictionary. She looked quite cross when she found that Ella had put 'For Nancy' in the front of Sherlock Holmes.

Then she stood back like I was a BAD SMELL Under Her Nose—while Cook tipped out my suitcase & threw all the sheets off my bed & turned the mattress over. But there was nothing they could object to there. So she told Cook to go thru the cupboards. That's when she spotted the paper with Blue Sky Motion Pictures at the top. I didn't put it back in my Journal after I found my writing had vanished but left it on top of the chest of drawers. (A big mistake.) She thundered 'What's that doing here?!'—as if it was the Crown Jewels.

My Diary of Detection! I was just waiting for them to discover it—convinced the next place they'd try looking was UNDER THE FLOORBOARDS. (If they ever read a crime book they'd know where to look.) I felt so shocked & horrified I was just shivering & trying not to cry.

Mrs B. said 'There's nothing else here.' As if she was Diserpointed not to find the best knives and some of her bracelets hidden away. Then Cook piped up 'I'd say she's spent the rest of what she took. I'd say she's been stealing from you ever since the start.'

How dare they! They have jumped to conclusions on NO EVIDENCE.

(Except the evidence of me with money in my hand.)

But when I tried to explain they wouldn't let me. Every time I opened my mouth Mrs Bryce snapped at me. 'I took you on—a chit of a girl without a clue! I trained you up and this is how you repay me!!'

Cook stood behind her looking pleased. If a grim old mouth like a rip in a sheet can look pleased.

I am so ANGRY my writing is coming out all shaky.

Then I had to pack my things up while Cook watched over me. She even watched while I got out of my uniform & into my own clothes so that I didn't steal a blasted apron off them! There was not A MOMENTS CHANCE to take my Journal out of its hidey-hole.

My hands were trembling so much that I couldn't get the suitcase catch done up. Everything fell out & I had to start all over again. I don't know how my legs carried me down 2 flites of stairs. Mrs Bryce was waiting in the hall. And worst of all there was GG, too. They had their heads together muttering. I expected him to say the Constable was on his way & make me stand there shaking in my shoes til I was ARRESTED.

But no. GG didn't speak to me. No one said a word about the Police. Mrs Bryce told me to GET OUT! Cook said 'Glad to see the back of that one' & shoved me into the night & slammed the door.

I don't know what they expected me to do—WALK home?

Mrs Bryce had never given me more than one weeks wages & I only had a few pennies left.

I suppose I should be glad they LET ME OFF like that. I don't suppose a Policeman would beleve me either.

The funniest thing—as I went out the gate Alfred drew up in the Motor Car. 'I forgot to hand this over' he said & gave me a big flat box. I hadn't seen him all day but next thing he said was 'Not staying—not being paid for this!' and the car took off again with a squeal & a stink of petrol. I didn't know what to make of that.

But I knew what was in the box. The Midnight Mermaid dress from Maisie Lockett. Mrs Bryce was not getting that dress! OVER MY DEAD BODY as Gran says. She never paid Maisie for it. Nor for the others neither!

It was getting DARK & starting to rain. I couldn't just walk all the way to London with my belongings over my shoulder like Dick Wittington. I wasn't a person in a story. I had to find somewhere to hide away for the night. I thoght the Vicar would probably side with Mrs Bryce if I went to him—but I knew they don't lock churches up so that's where I headed.

I'd got the dress box under one arm & my suitcase under the other. I must have stumbled into a tombstone in the dark cos next thing the suitcase bust open again. All my stuff scattered over the graves—getting wet & muddy & stuck with leaves. That's when Ella Otter found me. I gave her A BIT OF A SCARE—looming up at her so sudden out of the dark. (I was only picking up vests & knickers.)

She gave me a right scare too!

Now I'm here in her house. She's letting me sleep in the bedroom of their housekeeper who is away. It's nice & cosy with cushions & ~~embrod~~ embroyderies & pictures all round—lots are of Ella when she was little. NOT AT ALL like Cook's room at Cliffe Lodge!

The cat has made himself at home on the bed cover & is purring.

I told Ella EVERYTHING that happened today. She is a Good Listener. She said Mrs Bryce and GG definitly behaved suspiciously when they didn't summon the police to arrest me if they beleved I was a Theef. They just wanted an excuse to get rid of me—and did not want the Police poking their noses into their business! Why?

She agreed with me about the Mermaid Dress. I asked if she could get it back to Maisie somehow & she said I should keep it! IN LOO OF WAGES, she said. I had to point out it was Maisie who paid for the material & did the sewing & she didn't owe me any wages.

Ella got me to put the dress on—my own was soaking wet and all my other muddy things were draped about the room to dry. I didn't look much like a Mermaid and in the mirror my new short hair stuck up all round my head like a ginger HALO due to the damp. 'You look like an ANGEL' Ella said. Which was good of her (cos I looked more like a drowned rat).

Then she gave me this paper to write on. She knows about my Journal—I told her it was lost—& she says we'll get it back. I don't know who she means by WE.

Professor Otter doesn't know I'm here yet. Ella says he won't mind. (She seems quite certain about that.) She didn't want to disturb him tonight as he is busy Writing A Book.

Now I'm here writing mine. But it doesn't feel the same. I can just picture my Journal up there under the floorboards—and how there are pages & pages of stuff that Mrs Bryce & Cook & GG MUST NEVER GET THEIR HANDS ON.

LATER

Ella just came up with hot milk. (Someone waiting on ME for a change!)

I've written a quick note home & one to Alfred too—Ella will get that to him tomorrow somehow. I would hate Alfred to think bad of me.

Now I just need a way to get home. (Still haven't thoght of one.)

But I need to get my Journal back first & I haven't thoght how to do that either.

Then Ella said I couldn't go home. 'Not yet. We've got a case to solve, Nancy!'

MODERN HAIR

MERMAID DRESS!

High Gables,
The Green,
Seabourne,
Sussex.

Dear All,

If you look carefully at the address above you will see that I am not at Mrs Bryce's house any longer. I am at another house on The Green with Professor Otter and his daughter Ella. It's a long story. I think if it was a book like the ones you send me, Aunty Bee, it would be called 'Mistaken Identity'! I will explain all when I can. I may be home v. soon after you get this letter.

Please do not WORRY. (I know I am always putting that.) But you must not. I am just like a rubber Beach Ball and bounce back from everything.

Your affeckshunate daughter—grand-daughter—& neece,

Nancy xxx

Alfred—

I expect by now you have heard from
Mrs Bryce & Cook that I am

a LIAR and a THEEF.

Please don't beleve them! I did not steal any
money for myself.
They are the ones who are THEEVES if you
ask me. I can explain it all. Speak to Ella Otter
next door—she will have more news. I hope you
DO beleve me.

Nancy Parker

50 MIDNIGHT FEAST

NANCY'S JOURNAL

I swear I had not SLEPT A WINK when Ella poked her head around the door.

'Listen! We're going to have a Midnight Feast' and she made us count the chimes of the church clock. Which was only 11. 'Late enuff' she said & dragged me off to her bedroom which is big & untidy with lots of clothes flung about. (Reminded me of Mrs Bryce.)

I asked what a Midnight Feast was & Ella said 'It's something they have in Boarding Schools. That boy at the Vicarage knows all about them—lucky pig!'

That's the boy I told her to investigate. She said the matter was resolved now & came to a HAPPY CONCLUSION—more or less.

There was a heap of food on her bed including Sardines, butter, Ginger Snaps, some sticky lemon drops, a drum of Cocoa & the end of a loaf. She said 'What we do is have a secret picnic—and no grown-ups must hear us or they will come & interfere!' But there was only her dad & she'd already said that when he was DEEP IN HIS WORK nothing could disturb him.

Ella had not got anything to open the sardine tin with so I buttered torn-off bits of bread & sprinkled cocoa powder on them instead. Not as good as Cook's party food—but never mind!

Then we went over The Case.

Ella's Theory about Connie Bryce and GG being FAKES:—

They've both made up things about their past.

GG pretended to be a war hero & lied about flying air-o-planes. She told me he stole the story off a real air ace.

Which means—what else has he lied about?

Those photos on the Mrs Bryce's mantelpiece could be of anyone at all. Not her mother & father or Mr Bryce. Ella showed me a picture of a girl & a dog—I thoght it was her when she was younger—but she said she paid sixpence for it in town & it was a Complete Stranger. Which just shows how you can make people see what they expect to see.

Mrs B. wants to look like a nice kind genuine sort of person. Ella said that was sy-coll-ogy. If someone looks pretty and acts charming—everyone assumes they're as GOOD INSIDE as they are outside.

Mrs B. pretends to be rich & puts on a great show so that everyone bileves it.

When in fact she's cheated me & she cheated Maisie Lockett & just about every shopkeeper in Seabourne.

I had a shivery-cold feeling then & remembered my first impresshuns of her. I told Ella I suspected she took me on because I was YOUNG & IGNORANT (= cheap and easy to fool!) It was my very first time in service so I didn't know what to expect. Or how to stand up for myself. And she beleved I had no family to stick up for me either.

Alfred's young as well—it's his first proper showfer job.

The only one who knows a <u>Bit About Life</u> is Cook and she has been with Mrs Bryce for years. Like Alfred said—Cook promised to look after her. Stick with her thru THICK & THIN—and never gossip.

But Ella saw thru her! She knew right away that Mrs Bryce's laugh was FAKE. Me—I just thoght she was feeling nervous about such a big party. 'That probably means you're kinder than I am' Ella said. I told her she was kind too or she wouldn't have taken me in like this.

She said 'I did it cos we are frends!' (I felt all warm again then.)

I said 'But housemaids aren't usually friends with posh girls. It's not PROPER.' Ella just shrugged at that & said 'Father never worries about doing things the proper way. Who cares what people think? They can just put it down to him being American—and not teaching me <u>stuffy</u> English habits!'

We ate all the Ginger Snaps next & the Lemon Drops. Ella put on a hat that was lying about (she put it on all sideways & silly)—& a sash—& waved a stick about. It's what she's got to wear for her new School but she hates it and she's sure she will hate the school and everyone in it.

I told her about my old school & how they didn't know what to do with you once you had learnt all the lessons. Turns out Seabourne Grammar School for Girls is quite the opposite. There is a LIBARY & a SIENCE LAB & a garden with A POND so they can study the things that live in it.

I said I should not mind wearing a Maroon-and-Mustard uniform if it meant I could learn interesting things & not be stuck in a classroom with kids much younger & the only books you got to read were smelly & old & falling to bits.

(Tho I have to say that a lot of the books here in Ella's house are like that!)

Ella was quiet then as if she was thinking. I added 'There are bound to be other new girls starting. Girls who never had a Midnight Feast or solved a crime.' That made her smile.

So then she said:

'I wonder who Connie Bryce truly is?

And which one—if any—is her real name?'

'She could have a whole string of false names' I replied. Cos I'd remembered something else. Got the shivery feeling again.

There was something Cook said weeks ago—I'm sure I noted it down—about calling herself Treadgold—not being called Treadgold.

And there were those newspaper clippings Cook kept that might be about Mrs Bryce's family. The one I had was about a young woman who tricked her employer out of money—but got off because the old woman liked her so much. I couldn't recall the name. Ella wanted to read it & I had to say it was in my Diary of Detection. Under the floorboards.

We've got to get it back!

51 A PROPER PLAN

Mr Cheeseman was out on parish visits. Quentin raced through the page of maths he had left. Old Cheesy must be going soft, he thought. The sums were definitely getting easier. Although the answer to the last one came out at 197¾. Quentin didn't think 197¾ could ever be the right answer to a sum. He shrugged, and moved on to Geography. Mr Cheeseman had given him a detailed map of the local area and he was supposed to find and note down the co-ordinates of the following items: a marsh, a pine-wood, a hill over 300 feet high, a railway station, an airfield. He knew what he was going to start with: the airfield.

A large vehicle heaved itself through the vicarage gateway and crunched over the gravel. Quentin recognized the station van. Mrs Cheeseman stuck her head around the study door and said, in her usual firm way, 'Quentin. Out here, please.'

The driver was just setting down an enormous parcel in the porch. Mrs Cheeseman squeezed Quentin's shoulder.

'It was that last postcard from your mother,' she murmured, as the driver went back to his van. 'The one that said they were enjoying the South of France so much that they were going to stay on another few weeks and had just found a delightful house to rent. I decided to write to your parents' housekeeper and ask if she would be so kind as to send your summer clothes . . . and anything else that she thought you might find useful.'

The driver was wrestling something else out of the van now, an awkward shape that seemed to be stuck. At last, a bicycle emerged, a bike with a black frame and silvery trims to its black mudguards. Quentin's own bicycle.

'You're a whizz, Mrs Cheese!' he found himself exclaiming. He had a thought. 'May I cycle over to Ella Otter's house—right away, this minute—and show her?'

'Of course, Quentin. Of course you may,' Mrs Cheeseman beamed back. 'You know—we only want you to be happy!'

He had forgotten how hard it was to cycle over gravel. Under the gaze of Mrs Cheeseman, the van driver, and the big ginger cat, he crunched and wobbled away as slowly as if he was cycling through school rice pudding.

Professor Otter was eating a late breakfast of toast and marmalade at the kitchen table, nose deep in the morning paper. Ella watched him.

'Father . . . ?' she began.

'I know that tone of voice, Ella. It means you want something.'

'Only information, Father.'

'Information is a good thing.'

'Exactly. So, Father, did you think Mr Gommershall's movie scheme a good investment?'

Professor Otter chuckled. 'Ella, I know nothing about the business of film-making. It's much too modern for my tastes. I really don't know why the chap thought I had any money to invest.'

'Because of the Otter railway millions, and motor-car millions!'

'Oh, those. Those belong to my cousins.'

'But if you did—would you? Because Mr Gommershall said it's the coming thing. He might be right. Miss Dearing was excited about it. And Major Corcoran.'

Professor Otter put down the newspaper, but only to fold it to the crossword. 'If you want to invest your pocket money, Ella, please do. It would be a useful experiment for you.'

'I don't suppose GG will be interested in pocket money.'

'GG?'

'That's what Connie—Mrs Bryce—calls him.'

'You seem to know a lot about them.'

Ella changed tack. 'What did you think of Mrs Bryce?'

'A charming lady.' Professor Otter licked one of the blunt kitchen pencils Mrs Prebble kept for writing shopping lists, and began filling in the crossword.

'Father, I believe that's another of your white lies.'

'I was being polite. I suspect Mrs Bryce is one of those social butterflies who feels she isn't alive unless she's at a party. Right at the centre of one.'

'You wouldn't care to marry her?'

'Marry her!' Professor Otter laughed again, and threw

aside the pencil and the paper.

Ella said lightly, 'Mrs Prebble thinks she's husband-hunting.'

'Enough nonsense, Ella. I'm off to my study, to get on with the serious business of the day.' He strolled into the hall, then called back over his shoulder, 'I believe you have a visitor.'

Ella rushed out, expecting to see Nancy in the hallway, come in search of breakfast. But it was Quentin Ives, propping a bicycle against the porch. As she watched him, a plan began to form in her head. A better plan than any she had thought of so far.

52 ENEMY TERRITORY

Ella said, 'I ought to do it because Nancy's my friend.'

But Quentin said, 'No, I ought to do it. If anyone finds me there they'll think it's because I'm the burglar. The robberies only started after I arrived at The Green—and very few people know the truth of it.'

Ella and Quentin exchanged a solemn look. 'It will be better if we both go.'

'But not until the coast is clear,' said Nancy. 'Cook'll be extra busy without a housemaid. Let's hope Mrs Bryce goes out.'

They didn't have long to wait. Ella kept watch from the landing window. Soon Alfred came out and readied the car, Mrs Bryce appeared, and they drove away.

Ella dashed downstairs. The others were sitting at the kitchen table, Nancy looking anxious and Quentin eager.

'There's no time to lose,' Ella said. 'Just our luck it's a summer's day and not a dark and stormy night. But we must strike now!'

As Nancy predicted, the back door was unlocked. It swung inwards without a sound.

'Handy for burglars,' Ella hissed into Quentin's ear. 'Didn't they listen to Dozy Jim's advice!?'

Ella led the way. No noise from the kitchen. In fact, everything was deathly quiet. Only the sound of a clock ticking as they crept into the entrance hall.

At the foot of the stairs she whispered, 'What if he's here?'

'Who?'

'That fellow GG.'

'If he's here, he's making no sound.'

'What if he's snoozing on the sofa? Or busy in his office? I can never hear Father when he's working in his study. If you went very close you might hear the scratch of his pen. That's all.'

They stared at each other, aghast.

Ella asked, 'Did you see him leave?'

'No. But I didn't see any sign of him here, either.'

'I'll keep look-out downstairs. Are you sure you know where to go?'

Quentin nodded.

Ella watched him test the first stair. Nancy had told them that nothing squeaked or creaked, but the house was extraordinarily quiet right now. The lightest footfall might sound like thunder. Quentin tried the next, and then the next, and soon he was at the halfway landing. She watched him disappear round the turn in the stair.

She found that she was holding her breath.

Stealthy as a stalking tiger, silent as a mouse, John Horsefield climbed the winding stair.

With Professor Otter's old knapsack on his back, Quentin arrived at the top floor slightly breathless. His heart was pounding. He felt that at any minute it might jump right out of his chest. He was on a real mission, though, with real risk: retrieving vital documents from deep within enemy territory.

The sun shone in through the landing window, tinting the paintwork with gold. He wished it was night-time, too. He could have brought a torch, and blackened his face with engine grease, and flitted from shadow to shadow.

The first door on the right: it was even brighter inside, as there were two windows. One looked over the side of the house. Quentin peered down. The ginger cat was there, sitting in the middle of the driveway, its back leg stuck straight up in the air and washing its bottom.

Time is of the essence, John Horsefield popped up in his head to remind him.

Nancy's journal was hidden beneath a loose floorboard, and the loose floorboard was under the bed. It was a mean little bed; he could shift it easily. It was a mean room altogether, Quentin thought, even compared to his bedroom at the vicarage, which was hardly luxurious.

Time is of the essence! John Horsefield said again. *With practised hands, he felt for the loose board, and eased it out.*

But Quentin couldn't find a loose board. They all felt the same! He was in the right room, wasn't he? He was sure he'd followed Nancy's directions. But under pressure his brain didn't seem to work very well. He was sweating now. His fingers were slippery. The sun made it hot and stuffy and both windows were shut tight.

Nancy said the first door on the right; a room with

two windows, one overlooking the garage drive. It had to be this one.

He went over the area again, inch by inch. And, at last, something gave.

The clock's ticking was beginning to annoy Ella. And the length of time Quentin was taking. She would have been much quicker!

She gazed up the yards of shining banister rail. To think that Nancy polished it all, and swept all that stair-carpet. She stared hard at the half-landing where Quentin had disappeared, willing him to materialize. Nothing.

She glanced back down the hallway, a rapid survey, just as a good look-out should. Be alert to all quarters.

A door was—silently—inching—open!

Ella froze.

Nothing happened. No one stepped out. No one called, 'Hey! What the devil are you up to?'

And then she saw it.

A black nose, not far from the floor.

Sausage shoved at the door once more and eased his whole self out. He made his way towards Ella, whining with pleasure. He clearly remembered the party treats.

She bent and stroked his ears. 'I think we'd better shut you back in before you give the game away,' she breathed.

She carried him into the room he'd slipped out of. A dog basket was tucked under the desk. Sausage allowed himself to be put into it, but looked too wriggly to settle.

Ella straightened up and glanced around.

The room was some kind of study. There was a typewriter, and papers all over the desk. In one corner stood a tripod with a big wooden box on it, a handle on the side. GG's moving-picture camera! Perhaps he wasn't a fake after all. Framed photographs hung all round the walls. Ella peered at them one by one. People she didn't recognize, although from their delighted smiles it looked as though they expected to be recognized. Film stars? On the desk was a shot of what it must look like when you were making a film. She peered harder. Still no one she recognized, not even GG himself. If he was such an important person, why wouldn't he appear where they were making the film? Giving instructions, pointing the camera, bawling through a megaphone?

She went back to the desk and examined the papers. Headed sheets like the one Nancy said she'd stolen, and a fountain pen patterned in red marble. She slipped it into her skirt pocket. There were other papers covered in writing—printing, rather. She picked up the top one and began to read.

In his basket, Sausage sat up very straight and gave a sharp little bark.

Ella heard a voice, out in the hallway.

'Hoi! What the devil are you up to!?'

Quentin looked out of the side window again. He had the journal now. He was supposed to put it in the knapsack Ella had given him and drop the whole thing down into the privet hedge. 'You mustn't be found with it on you, if you get caught,' Ella had said. 'We'll retrieve it later, once we're safely out.'

But the hedge was a very long way down. He might miss. His aim was improving these days, but that was with a cricket ball, not a clumsy knapsack. It might land on the driveway and split apart, Nancy's journal with it. Pages of secret writing would scatter to the four winds: crucial evidence fluttering away. And what a noise it would make landing! And how conspicuous it would look as it fell!

Ella's plan was a bad plan, Quentin thought. John Horsefield might manage it but he, Quentin, was not up to the job. He slid the journal into the knapsack, hoisted it on his shoulder and made off swiftly, silently, down the first flight of stairs.

The door was still partly open. Ella could see Quentin in the hallway, stuck in mid-stride like someone in a game of musical statues (one of the ghastly games Mrs Cheeseman always made them play at the vicarage Christmas party). For a split-second, their eyes met.

'You, boy! What the devil are you doing in here?'

In the dumb pause that followed Ella could hear (apart from that blasted clock!) the creak of old boots.

Quentin held up one hand, palm out. Ella could see it was a signal meant for her. Don't move.

Sausage sidled up to her ankles. Ella wondered how she could keep him still and quiet beside her. She felt in her pocket—coming across the fountain pen—and found a broken bit of shortbread at the bottom, along with loads of sugary crumbs. Without taking her eyes off Quentin she dropped it beside her and heard Sausage's satisfied gulp.

And then Quentin spoke. His voice was surprisingly steady, and very polite.

'I rang the bell,' he said, 'but no one came. I wonder that you didn't hear it. Then I found that the front door wasn't quite closed. Your maid must be rather forgetful.'

'Our maid!' the other voice spat.

'I really didn't mean to intrude. I've been out for a hike, and I wonder if I could beg a glass of water. I got a bit lost, you see, and it's very hot and I'm very thirsty –'

Ella heard them retreating down the hall, Quentin's polite schoolboy tones and Cook's slightly grumpy ones intertwining.

'Just water? I've got some lemonade in the pantry, keeping cool.'

'Oh, lemonade would be jolly nice. . .'

'There might be cake to spare besides. No point in it going to waste.'

Ella saw Quentin's hand on the kitchen door before it was firmly shut behind him. Leaving her free to make her escape.

53 RED HERRINGS

NANCY'S JOURNAL

I have got it back! I never thought I would but now it is HERE—safe!

I've just read parts of it out loud to Ella and that boy Quentin Ives. (I had to ask him how to spell his name.) Not the parts where I said rude things about them. They are good kids, as it turns out.) I showed them GG's note with the air-o-plane sketch, and where I put that my writing on the Blue Skies paper had quite vanished. I found that old clipping about a sneaky girl called Mary Constance Dyer. We've got so much evidence now—but what is it EVIDENCE OF?

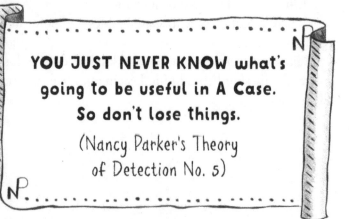

YOU JUST NEVER KNOW what's going to be useful in **A Case. So don't lose things.**

(Nancy Parker's Theory of Detection No. 5)

Ella was the first one back from their Mission to rescue my Journal—all alone & empty-handed. She said that

Cook had got hold of the boy but she didn't think it was A TRAP—more of an accident. We could only wait & see.

So we sat and waited, dead scared. Every so often Ella would jump up & go & look over the hedge & listen in case she could hear anything coming from Cliffe Lodge. SCREAMS OF PAIN or CRIES FOR HELP. Anything. But all was quiet.

Then suddenly he was back—looking like he'd been dragged thru a hedge. Cook had sent him out by the Golf Course path cos he told her he was a on a hike and got lost. So he had to sneak round the back way to Ella's house—but the only way is thru a field with A BULL in it. He had to cross it without getting a DEADLY WOUND from the bull himself. Quentin said nothing much but I could tell he was quietly proud.

The main thing—apart from the fact that he did not get GORED—is that he had my Journal safe in his bag. Also a package of cake Cook gave him (somewhat squashed.) She wanted to put the cake in his bag to make sure it didn't get squashed & he had to fend her off—or she would have found my Journal in it!!

Ella made us hot chocolate to celebrate The Success of The Mission. It felt strange eating Cook's cake RIGHT NEXT DOOR & quite unknown to her. I don't think it felt so strange to the others.

(Also the weather is rather hot for hot chocolate. But I did not object.)

The success of the mission is as follows:

My Journal is safe!!! If Cook or Mrs Bryce found it I'm sure they would have been v. angry and then destroyed it.

Quentin found out more VITAL INFORMATION about Cook. She told him how she had a little boy of her own once. She had no husband (!) & had to work—so the boy was looked after by her own mother. She said she was in service with a kind family but she hardly ever saw him—and then he died very young!

This must be the infant I saw in that photo & the old woman is her mother. (Even tho I loathe Cook I can see this is an awful thing to happen to her.)

We agreed that this is:

why she looks so grim

& why she has a soft spot for boys—just as Alfred thought! (It does not explain tho why she disliked me.)

The kind family must mean Mrs Bryce's mother—the one she made that promise to, to always keep an eye on Mrs B.

I don't really like to put it down here but a word keeps running thru my head. The word is FOOLISH.

I have just read my Journal right the way thru & I can see where I may have been foolish. Where I may have followed Red Herrings like in every detective book I've ever read.

Red Herrings = false trails that lead you off in the wrong direction.

I can see that reading 'Scream Blue Murder' might have made me dwell on the idea of bumping off husbands & 'A Taste For Killing' might have made me think too much of poisonings. I have read a lot of books where the person with the grim face & manner was the One Who Done IT. The pictures on the book jackets certainly give that impression.

But now I know what it is like to be on the wrong end of mistaken beliefs. Mrs Bryce is sure I am a THEEF and a LIAR—because she only looked at the surface. It feels awful to be an Honest Person and have some people truly beleve you are Dis-honest. (Even if you no longer think those people are Very Nice.)

One thing I held against Cook was that she seemed much too interested in nasty stories in the newspaper. But what about Aunty Bee and me? We love a good crime story too. It doesn't make us Criminals—far from it. That is as far as my forgiving thoghts about Cook will go. She was still horrid to me.

Ella said she had an idea & dashed off to see Miss Dearing—of all people—and Quentin said he better nip back to the vicarage to prove he hadn't been knocked off his bike by a motorcar.

So I came up to Mrs Prebble's room to lie low & write this.

The doorbell just rang. If a bell rings now I feel it's my job to answer it! But not here.

I hope it's not the POLICE. Or anyone else looking for me. I shall creep out on the landing and take a peep—

54 TOP SECRET

Ella ran full-tilt down the path to Apple Cottage. It would be the first time she'd seen Miss Dearing face-to-face and on her own ever since she'd managed to lose the rosebud bag. But—just as Nancy had said—the thieving magpie was a mere trifle compared to what was going on now.

She found Miss Dearing in her scarlet driving cape, harnessing the donkey.

'Ella—just the person I—'

Ella interrupted her. 'Miss Dearing, have you put any money into the Blue Sky Motion Picture Company?'

Miss Dearing looked flustered, then beamed. 'I suppose it isn't top secret, is it? Not when so many of us have been—'

'Did you sign any papers?'

'Yes, of course. Mr Gommershall is very business-like and organized.'

'May I see them?'

'Ella, you are eleven years old. My private financial matters have nothing to do with you!'

Ella hopped impatiently from foot to foot. 'You trusted me before, Miss Dearing—on that other private matter.'

'Yes, and look how that turned out!'

'It turned out perfectly well,' Ella reminded her. Even if not quite as Miss Dearing had planned. 'Now, please can I see those papers?'

'I'm about to take Pancho for a drive.'

'It's very urgent!'

'I really don't see . . .' Miss Dearing tutted, but she tied the donkey to a post and led Ella towards the house. She opened the door carefully. 'You may find it a little stuffy in here, Ella. I've been keeping all the windows closed. It's poor Marius, you see. I couldn't bear him shut up in that cage any longer—now he has the freedom of the house.'

A rush of air and whirring black wings came at Ella. She ducked. Marius landed on the kitchen table and glared at her, head on one side.

'I keep all my papers in here,' Miss Dearing called from the next room. 'It's really very exciting, at my time of life, to be invited to help a new art form, a twentieth-century art form, on its way. I was born in the age of the crinoline, you know. Now there are motor cars, aeroplanes - and moving pictures! Who would have ever imagined it?'

She brought out a battered tin box and unlocked it. Her fingers shook with excitement. 'Look, here is my Certificate of Investment. I believe I was the very first one to go to Mr Gommershall and say yes!'

Ella grabbed the piece of paper that Miss Dearing was unfolding. There had been a similar document on Mrs Bryce's desk. At the top it said BLUE SKY MOTION PICTURES. Below were paragraphs of small close print and at the foot space for a sum of money and signatures.

Ella swallowed when she saw how much money had been typed in.

'Is this what you gave Mr Gommershall?'

'Not gave, Ella dear, invested. In the foremost art form of the—'

'I know, but it's an awful lot.'

'All my savings, in fact.'

'Everything? Because from what I can see here you haven't signed it yet, and nor has he. That means you're not committed to the deal.'

Miss Dearing grabbed the paper back. Her face was as white as a church candle.

'We signed it days ago—when I handed him my money.'

Ella pulled GG's red marble pen from her pocket. 'Did he get you to sign it with this?'

Miss Dearing nodded. They both stared at the paper. The space where the signatures of both Miss Dearing and Guy Gommershall should have been was completely blank.

55 GETTING AWAY

When John Horsefield was on the trail of vicious criminals he wouldn't bother telling anyone he'd not be home to tea.

That's what Quentin was thinking as he skidded his bike to a halt in the vicarage gateway, spraying gravel.

'I had some lunch with Ella Otter,' he explained to Mrs Cheeseman, 'and they've invited me back to tea.'

'That's lovely, Quentin. I'm so pleased you're making friends at last. But what about your lessons?'

'Um, Professor Otter was there too, and we— and we talked about archaeology for ages. It was very educational.'

'Splendid, Quentin,' Mrs Cheeseman said. 'Mr Cheeseman wants a word with you. A very important word. He's written to your parents—'

Oh, no! thought Quentin. That was the last thing he needed. But he wasn't going to let anything get in the way of his mission. 'Can't stop now, Mrs Cheese—must get back.'

He rushed away down the passageway before she could object.

'Mr Cheeseman thinks you're doing very well,' she called after him. 'But he feels you would do even better if you stayed on here and attended a day school, rather than return to your old . . .'

Quentin scarcely heard her. He banged the front door shut.

Mrs Bryce's motor car was back in the driveway. Quentin was surprised to see her chauffeur, in full uniform, cycling off rapidly in the direction of Seabourne. He turned his own bike to follow and pedalled hard to catch up. He might get some useful information out of him to take back to Ella's. John Horsefield would know how to engage a chap in easy chat and soon have all he needed, and the fellow would suspect nothing.

'I say—is this the way into town?' he asked as he drew alongside.

Alfred nodded. 'That's where I'm going.'

'Just got my bicycle this morning,' Quentin said. 'Much better than walking.' He eyed Alfred's uniform. 'Not as good as driving though.'

Alfred grunted.

It was uphill work, this easy chat. Quentin tried again. 'Thought you'd be driving a car in an outfit like that?'

'I've had my orders, to leave the motor and ride into Seabourne with a message. Even though I've been there already today, ferrying milady about.'

'That doesn't make sense.'

Alfred grunted again. 'I'm not paid to make sense of it. Orders is orders.'

'I could take the message for you. Who's it to?'

Alfred kept on pedalling and looking straight ahead.

'Now why would you do that? When you don't even know your way into town?'

'I—um—I like to be helpful.' That sounded very lame. Just as Quentin was thinking up another question, Alfred put on a sudden burst of speed and shot away, calling back, 'Bye now. Don't get lost!'

Quentin sat down on a roadside bank to get his breath back. His bicycle lay on the ground, the back wheel still spinning. His insides were spinning, too. It wasn't quite true what he'd told Mrs Cheeseman about lunch—or tea. All he'd had since breakfast was hot chocolate and cake, and now they were swirling queasily round in his stomach.

He picked up his bike and was just climbing on when a figure appeared in the distance. A familiar figure . . . tall and thin, stumping along grimly, getting nearer all the time. It was the cook from Cliffe Lodge—and she carried a suitcase in her hand!

He thought back to the scene in the kitchen that morning. The room was very clean and tidy, with no sign of cooking going on—and when the cook fetched the cake-plate from the pantry the shelves behind her were bare. Of course—everything was being packed up. They'd got rid of Nancy and now they were ready to flee.

When he glanced back up the lane, shading his eyes against the afternoon sun, the figure was nowhere to be seen! She couldn't just have vanished.

He pedalled hard up the hill, retracing his route—and found a turning that he'd missed when he was following

Alfred. A narrow, shady lane dipped away, and a leaning signpost, half-hidden in the ivy, pointed to 'Station ½ mile'. It must be Seabourne Halt, on the branch-line he'd traced that morning on Mr Cheeseman's local map. And stumping away through the shadows was Mrs Bryce's cook. She was making her getaway.

56 PROOF

As Ella dashed in at her own gateway, Nancy opened the front door. She was still clutching her Journal, as if she would never let it go.

Ella pushed past her, gasping, 'Guy Gommershall's a cheat and I've got proof! Where's my father? I need to speak to him.'

'He went out,' Nancy said. 'A telegram boy came to the house and then your dad rushed off. He left this lying on his desk.'

She thrust the piece of paper into Ella's hand. It was a single creased sheet with words glued in strips across it.

> CHECKED AS YOU REQUESTED. STOP. GUY
> GOMMERSHALL UNKNOWN IN HOLLYWOOD STOP.
> INVESTMENT HAH! STOP. TAKE MY ADVICE
> COUSIN STOP! STOP. COSWAY OTTER. STOP.

Ella had to read it twice. At first the strange staccato telegram language confused her, but she knew who had sent it. 'Cosway Otter—that's Father's cousin in California.'

'He's been making enquiries for your dad,' Nancy said. 'Investigating Guy Gommershall. Seeing if all that boasting about famous film stars was true.'

Ella frowned. 'But Father never intended to put any money in Blue Sky Motion Pictures. He told me I could, if I wanted to. He said it would be a good experiment.'

'Sounds as if he thought it was chancy all along.'

'It was. It is. GG signed certificates for people who gave him their money, but they're worthless. Look at this!' Ella extracted from her pocket another crumpled sheet of paper.

Nancy glanced at it. 'There's no signatures there.'

'Exactly! Whatever was written has disappeared.'

'Just like on the bit of notepaper I stole.'

'He must use some kind of vanishing ink.'

'I've heard of invisible ink—'

'Well, this is the opposite. It looks clear and black at first—and then it fades away.'

'So no one can prove he ever had any money off them! So that's what they were up to!'

'It's all a trick—a very elaborate one.'

'That's why she made friends with everyone she could find who had a bit of money, and he got them excited about his scheme.' Nancy shook her head. 'So there won't be any film . . .'

'And there won't be any money—unless we can get some of it back. Poor Miss Dearing's handed over her life savings.'

'I know where Mrs Bryce keeps her cash—in a

wooden box painted with flowers. And I know where she hides the key.'

'Her car wasn't in the driveway. She must still be out,' Ella said. 'Come on! We'll have to be quick.'

For once all the doors of Cliffe Lodge were locked, all the windows shut. Nancy and Ella went from window to window, peering in. All neat and tidy, impersonal. Nobody there.

'It looks exactly the same as ever,' said Ella. 'Do you think they've flown?'

'No! Mrs Bryce is having a big dinner party tomorrow. Loads of people are invited.'

'But you said the pantry was half-empty. It's completely empty now. I think that dinner party is just another trick—to make people think Mrs Bryce and GG were going to be here, while all along they've been planning to run.'

Ella climbed down from the window ledge outside Cook's room. 'Her spare boots are gone—that's all I can make out.'

'Never was much to see,' said Nancy. She shivered, despite the warm day. 'Would they really slip away, just like that?'

They came to the morning room window.

'I hid in here, while Quentin did his marvellous bluff.' Ella pressed her face to the glass. 'The camera's still there. Surely GG wouldn't leave a valuable item like that, would he?'

'Might be just another thing they bought with no

intention of paying the bill.' Nancy peered in beside her. 'Looks like the pictures are still on the walls.'

'You know, anyone could buy photos of film stars and scribble all over them—"With love and kisses to darling Guy"!'

'I was taken in,' said Nancy.

'So was everyone! That's the point—and it's such an easy trick. Like Mr Bryce really being some poor man from Surrey called Leonard. Connie didn't much care when he got broken—that's another thing you put in your diary.'

'I did.'

Nancy cupped her hands around her eyes so that she could see in better. 'The cash box isn't there! She always keeps it on her desk.'

She and Ella stared at each other in horror. 'They have gone!'

'Who's gone?' puffed Quentin, hurtling his bike to a stop on the empty driveway.

'Mrs Bryce and GG—with everyone's money!'

Quentin wiped sweat from his forehead. 'The cook's gone too. I've just seen her, heading for the station.'

Ella grabbed Nancy's free hand and squeezed hard. 'No wonder she had hardly any belongings. She knew she was never going to stay. All the clues are there,'—she tapped the red cover of Nancy's journal—'in your diary of detection!'

'It was down to observation,' said Quentin.

'Instinct,' said Ella.

'Psychology, you mean,' Nancy reminded her. 'But we're too late.'

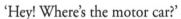

'Hey! Where's the motor car?'

The shout from The Green made them all look round. Alfred was speeding towards them.

'She's taken it, hasn't she? My uncle will skin me alive!' He nodded at Quentin. 'It started me thinking, what you said. I smelled a rat. Smelled a bigger one when I got to the grocer's to give him my message and he didn't know what I was on about. "What big order for tomorrow?" It was nonsense, just a ruse to get me out the way. Did any of you see her go?' He looked around their faces, as if seeing them properly for the first time, and gaped at Nancy. 'What are you doing here? Thought you'd be back in London by now.'

'Mrs Bryce got me out the way, too—but I never really left. Didn't you read my note?'

'What note?'

Ella was shouting, 'Never mind the car! They've conned everyone out of their savings and we've got the evidence to prove it.' She began pulling out the contents of her pockets. 'Here's the telegram—and here's the false document. Oh, wait, that's not—' She scrabbled at a square of folded paper. 'Sorry, here's your note, Nancy. Somehow—in all the excitement—I forgot.' She stopped. Her hand had encountered something else. Grinning, she flourished it in the air—GG's red fountain pen.

Alfred huffed and puffed, 'They're not getting away with it. I'm going to fetch the police.'

'They could be miles away by now,' said Quentin.

'They'll be driving back to London,' Nancy said. 'London's big enough to disappear in.'

'It's hopeless.'

Everyone fell silent.

In the sudden quiet a familiar summery buzz droned on the air. High above them the aeroplane that towed the red banner—VISIT SUNNY SEABOURNE!—was trailing its way home.

As clear as day Nancy saw GG's little note to Mrs Bryce: *Almost there now. Blue Skies here we come!* It was nothing to do with the film—just getting away with the money.

'That's how they're going to escape! Guy Gommershall can fly a plane!'

'Or so he says,' muttered Ella.

'The airfield—of course!' cried Alfred. 'Mrs Bryce knows how to get there.'

'They can take a plane and hop over to France,' cried Quentin. 'They can go anywhere!'

'Not if we stop them.'

Alfred was climbing on to his bike. 'Constable Towner's not far away. It's cricket practice tonight.'

'Jim Towner?' cried Ella. 'Dozy Jim? We need someone more capable than that!'

'Jim's a start—he can raise the rest of 'em. No one's going to steal my uncle's motor car!'

Quentin said, 'I know the way to the airfield. I saw it on the map this morning—and I've got a photographic memory. More or less.'

Alfred called back over his shoulder, 'You go ahead and stall 'em. I'll meet you there.'

Nancy ran into the garage and heaved out The

Valiant, tucking her journal safely into its basket. 'I'm not leaving that behind.'

'Let's go.'

'What about Ella?'

'She could ride with one of us,' said Quentin. 'But it'd slow us down.'

'No—I've got another idea!' cried Ella. 'But first I must fetch something.' She flew back to her own house as if she had wings on her heels.

57 THE BICYCLE DASH

Nancy followed Quentin along a maze of lanes until she lost all sense of direction. Suddenly a wide flat field opened out before them.

'There it is!' Quentin shouted.

Nancy didn't know if he meant the aeroplane waiting ready on the long straight strip where the planes took off and landed, or Alfred's motor car, which she could see parked haphazardly on the grass nearby. Two suitcases were piled on the ground beside it and, on top, a small brown shape. A shape which danced round and round in circles and barked in excitement.

Nancy could see that someone was climbing up into the plane—someone in an elegant cream motoring coat—and someone else was helping them in. It was all so far away and the muscles in her legs were aching! The Valiant was heavier than Quentin's bike but she leaned forward over the handlebars and pedalled as hard as she could.

'Hey! You! Wait!' she yelled, but it felt as if her voice blew away with the wind.

Yet the brown shape on top of the suitcases turned and barked in her direction.

The elegant cream coat disappeared inside the

plane and the other figure—tall and striking in brown overalls and flying helmet—faltered halfway to the cases. Stopped and ran back to the plane. Climbed up and vaulted inside.

Quentin was ahead of Nancy, some way to her right. He had no time to think *swiftly, boldly*. He could see that the plane's propeller was beginning to turn. With a jolt the craft moved forward.

There was a long low aeroplane hangar off to one side, a bit like a barn, with a wide-open front. Someone lounged against the wall, watching the aeroplane manoeuvre on the runway. He had a rag in his hand and was wiping a wrench. He looked as if he had all the time in the world—and he hadn't glanced in Quentin's direction, not once. The mad bicycle dash might as well be invisible.

As Quentin drew nearer he recognized the reddened face.

'Mr Atwood! Over here! Mr Atwood. Reggie!' His bike swerved wildly as he waved one hand high in the air. 'You've got to stop that plane.'

The man turned. 'What's that?'

The plane was taxiing on the runway and Nancy was falling further behind. Quentin shouted as he reached the war hero, 'Must—stop—that—plane. They're going to get away. GG—he's a—crook!'

Reggie Atwood broke into a leisurely run, jogging beside him. He swung the wrench in one hand; the oily rag flapped in the other. 'It's Horsefield, isn't it? What's going on, old chap?'

Quentin's breath felt like knives in his chest. He could only gasp, 'Must—stop—plane. Then—explain.'

The war hero ran harder. He raised the rag and waved it like a banner. But the plane had already picked up speed. Its wheels began to lift.

Quentin and Nancy screeched wordless warnings.

The war hero shouted, 'Look out!'

On top of the abandoned cases, Sausage leapt up and down and yelped, in vain.

Charging right at the front of the plane, like Boadicea on her chariot, came Ella Otter. She whirled a hockey stick above her head. Miss Dearing, scarlet cape flying out like wings, held the reins of the red-and-yellow donkey cart. Pancho remembered his glory days when the Seabourne beach donkeys got it into their heads to stampede. His hooves banged like drums on the hard-packed ground. Miss Dearing let out a blood-curdling roar.

Ella flung her weapon.

They're just paper and glue and string, those planes. Reggie Atwood's words ran through Quentin's head.

They heard a crack and a stutter and the aeroplane— which had barely risen from the ground—bumped back to earth, veered to the left and stumbled to a halt. One wing dipped, the other rose. Through a gash in it, Ella could see the sky.

58 THE MOST MOMENTOUS DAY

NANCY'S JOURNAL

Well—that was the most Momentous Day I ever had!

My career in films may be IN RUINS but my career as a Detective has truly begun.

Ella just rushed in—furious—waving a copy of the 'Seabourne Herald' and shouting 'Guess who's got his picture on the front page? Only Dozy Jim! What utter rot!'

And there he was standing in front of the air-o-plane in his uniform as if stopping the Get-away was all down to him. He must have gone home first & changed out of his cricket clothes for the photo.

Ella is just cutting out the page so I can put it in here. She says she will have to get another to stick in her Anthropollogy Scrapbook.

Seabourne Herald 13th August 1920

FILM FRAUDS FOILED AT TAKE-OFF

Alerted to the possibility of fraud by the eminent local historian, Professor Mildmay Otter, Seabourne police made two arrests at Oxcoombe Airfield yesterday evening. Guy Gommershall, 28, and Mary Constance Dyer, 35, were stopped on the point of taking off in a stolen plane after a hair-raising chase.

Mr Gommershall and Miss Dyer (going under the name of Mrs Connie Bryce) were found to have incriminating documents and a large sum of money in their luggage. It appears that the pair extorted funds from local residents in the guise of setting up a company to make moving pictures, using the delightful setting of Seabourne.

Police Inspector Morgan, Sergeant Douglas and P.C. Towner hurtled to the scene, accompanied by Professor Otter, just in time to prevent the pair from leaving the country with their ill-gotten gains. Miss E. M. Dearing, a disappointed investor who witnessed the dramatic arrests, was taken from the airfield in a state of distress.

Not a single menshunn of Ella—or Quentin—or Alfred—or ME! The big black Police car turned up just as we stopped the plane. If it wasn't for us, Mrs Bryce and GG would have been soaring over the English Channel by then. She had to leave her luggage behind—and Sausage—but she'd got all the money with her.

I will never beleve what I read in the papers again.

Ella is cross cos they called her dad a Historian—not an Archaeologist. (I just looked up how to spell that!)

Miss Dearing was not distressed—or disappointed—she was FLAMING ANGRY and had to be restrained from whopping GG with the cart-whip. (Which she never uses on a blameless animal, she said, just leaves in the donkey-cart in case it comes in handy.) (It certainly did.)

No menshun either of all the EVIDENCE we'd gathered—GG's pen, all the bits of paper, that news clipping—& handed to the Police. Not this Journal, thank goodness. What's in here is speckulation, it turns out, not evidence.

I am still here at Ella's house while Mrs Prebble is away. Prof. Otter is going to write to Dad & Gran & Aunty Bee about me and ask Aunty Bee if she would like to come for a holiday.

Sausage is here too!! Poor thing, he was very sad to be abandoned. Miss Dearing offered to take him but felt her GEESE would spit at him every time he went outside. He couldn't stay indoors either because that Magpie she

keeps in the house would bully him. There was NOTHING FOR IT but to bring him here. The cat doesn't care for this arrangement. But Ella says that Bernard is so often out about his own business that it hardly matters what he thinks. The house is big enough for a cat and a dog—specially a small one.

Ella's dad says he has no opinion on the matter but last night we made a bonfire in the back garden & Prof. Otter cooked sausages on twigs in the flames. He gave the ones that were too burnt to the dog. Who didn't think they were too burnt. 'Sausages for Sausage', he said. 'Am I encouraging cannibalism?'

I didn't expect a porfessor to make A JOKE. (I beleve it was a joke.)

The more I think about Aunty Bee coming here the more exited I get. We'll go on the Prom & the Pier—at last—and have tea at the Cafe Splendide & ice creams at Marco's. We'll listen to the band and watch the Pierrot Show—but we are much too dignified to ride on the donkeys!

And I will be sure to take Aunty Bee into the church & show her the beautiful stained-glass window made by a Famous Artist (I can't recall his name). It was put there by Prof. Otter in memory of Ella's mother. But Ella kindly says it is really to remember anyone's mother.

I'll stop this now becos Ella says we have been asked to lunch at the Vicarage—me too! It will be odd to sit at a table and not be waiting on it. Quentin says if we are lucky we can eat in the garden & not in the Dining Room with all the paintings of olden-day vicars staring down at us & Mrs Cheeseman is a dab hand at pastry & the eggs come from Miss Dearing's hens.

I can hear Ella calling my name—makes a change, not to be summoned to do some chore or other—so I MUST DASH!!

ACKNOWLEDGEMENTS

I'd like to thank all the people who helped turn the sketchiest of ideas into such a delicious-looking book. Designer Holly Fulbrook and illustrator Chloe Bonfield who made wonderful sense of my vague and optimistic instructions; my editor Liz Cross for egging me on to more madness; Emma Young for helping me cut to the chase; Debbie Sims for editorial help, and the rest of the team at Oxford for their enthusiasm. Thanks also to my lovely agent Gaia Banks for her connoisseur's knowledge of crime fiction, and to Agatha Christie and Miss Marple for a certain sort of ink...

ABOUT THE AUTHOR

JULIA LEE

Julia Lee has been making up stories for as long as she can remember. She wrote her first book aged 5, mainly so that she could do all the illustrations with a brand-new 4-colour pen, and her mum stitched the pages together on her sewing machine. As a child she was ill quite a bit, which meant she spent lots of time lying in bed and reading (bliss!).

Julia grew up in London, but moved to the seaside to study English at university, and has stayed there ever since. Her career has been a series of accidents, discovering lots of jobs she didn't want to do, because secretly she always wanted to be a writer.

Julia is married, has two sons, and lives in Sussex.

ALSO BY JULIA LEE

*A plucky orphan, a dark family secret,
and a thrilling race against time . . .*

Clemency is utterly penniless and entirely alone, until
she's taken in by the marvellous Marvels—a madcap
family completely unlike her own. But it's a surprise
to them all when she's mysteriously bundled from the
house by the frightening Miss Clawe.

Concerned about Clemency's fate, the Marvels
set out to find her. Enlisting the help of some
not-quite-genuine Red Indians, it's a calamitous race
across the country. But Clemency's misadventures are
more dire than her rescuers suspect . . . will they
reach her in time?

ISBN: 9780192733672